Alice Dippleblack in

The

Jellybane

By
K. J. Bailey

Second Edition

This is a work of fiction. Names, characters, places, and incidents either are the products of the author's imagination or are used fictitiously. Any resemblance to actual persons, living or dead, businesses, companies, events, or locales is entirely coincidental.

ISBN: 978-0-9978858-2-8

minatek616@gmail.com

Chapter 1

Jellies

Alice slashes at the grass green jelly again and again, careful not to damage the precious core within. Jellies have no organs to pierce, no real flesh to rend, or even bones to break. The simple semitransparent hemispherical creatures only have three parts to them. First is their outer layer. This is the layer exposed to the air and is transparent like the rest. About as tough as supple leather, it serves to hold the creatures together. A pointed stick could pierce it, but would have trouble dealing much damage to the creature itself. Fortunately, Alice wields a sword, left to her by her father, and with it, she cuts away at the green blob. The plain broadsword easily slices through the outer layer of the creature, sending thick green goo flying out in wild arcs. The jelly creature itself wobbles with each blow, steadily shrinking as bits of it are strewn about.

The jelly within, for which such creatures are named, is the most dangerous part about the wild monsters. Given enough time, jellies, while slow and thought only a minor nuisance can in fact be rather devastating to anything they touch. The jelly is a digestive goop. Whenever the creatures manage to find organic matter, they allow it to be absorbed through their outer layer and into their viscous insides where the matter is dissolved. The more matter a jelly dissolves the bigger it becomes. Then it can split, forming two identical smaller jellies. Alice had seen them do this. Like all things the jellies did, it was a slow process but helped explain their continuous presence in the area.

As Alice swings her sword, she scatters more and more of the mildly corrosive goo until the monster is brought down from its original three feet in diameter, to less than the size of her head. She then lowers her weapon and takes an accomplished breath as she reaches in for her prize, the core stone. This is the third and most valuable part of the jelly. Each one that Alice has ever encountered has had one of the spherical core stones. These were generally the same color, if a bit darker, than the jelly itself. Though not actually hewn from the earth, these hard little pearl like treasures were what made the jellies worth the effort to hunt, at least for a young girl with few other talents. Valued for their simple beauty and faint glow, the cores were often used to decorate jewelry and other goods.

Alice shakes off the rest of the slime from her eyeball sized treasure. She then wipes it off on her tan trousers for good measure before putting it in her faded blue shoulder bag with the others. Once done, she takes up her bag and walks a few steps to a fairly goo free zone to plop down onto her rump. She drains what's left in a water skin hanging at her hip and takes a few deep breaths, forcing air slowly into her lungs rather than panting as her body wants her too. Once her breathing reaches a natural rate, she lifts her bag into her lap and grins at the day's work. "And you make six," she announces proudly. Six of the small orbs light the inside of her cloth shoulder bag with their mysterious radiance. She gives them a little shake, taking pleasure in hearing the hard surfaces tapping together as they settle. "I should be able to get enough to go on a new expedition with this," she proclaims aloud to no one.

Alice Dippleblack is a young Tokala, or anthropomorphic fox. Her fine fur coat is a bright orange-red. The two triangular ears atop her head look as if their very tips where dipped in black ink, just as her feet, hands, nose, and tail, though the later must have been dipped in a different well, for it was white as freshly fallen snow. Alice also has a streak of white fur that starts from her nose and coats the lower half of her cheeks before drifting down her throat. She wears what once had been a white blouse but now is more gray and brown with dirt where it isn't covered with green jelly stains. Her tan trousers are functional, if worn, with good deep pockets and a slit in the back for her long full tail to poke free from. Her feet are bare, allowing her toes to feel the sun warm grass while her tail flops about happily behind her as she admires her haul of cores.

Alice's sharp ears angle as they pick up the subtle sound of movement. Sky blue eyes look to see another green jelly slowly drifting along only a few yards away. She glances at the setting sun, making its way to the horizon, and in a second gauges the time, her remaining stamina, and the energy it will take to get back to the village. She smirks at the creature, "I think we can get in one more," and picks up her sword.

It was rare to encounter jellies so near each other this close to the village and it was an opportunity Alice did not want to pass up. She hefts the double-edged broadsword in both hands, neither of her slender arms quite ready to handle its full weight alone, and charges the jelly. The monster's only reaction is to wobble a bit at her high pitched battle cry, though Alice didn't think they had ears.

Jellies have no features, no face nor arms, and all of them look like gelatin that was molded to a hemispherical bowl then dumped out. The only noise they ever made was when they slid on a dry leaf or twig and it crinkled or crackled under them. As such, Alice's intimidating shout and ya!-ing was unlikely to affect the creatures, but it made the somewhat smaller than average girl feel brave and strong.

Like with every encounter, Alice is careful to avoid hitting the core while knocking away as much of the goo as she can. She had tried before, and so she knew it was possible to cut a slit in the outer layer, then reach in through the thick jelly and grab the core. But as she had discovered, the viscous ooze irritates the skin and is difficult to clean from fur. And whacking at them was more fun besides. She slashes enthusiastically until its safe enough to reach for the stone, this one not as big as the last. As jellies dissolve matter their gelatinous forms grow, this is true for the cores as well and so one can generally expect larger cores from larger jellies. This one wasn't all that big but didn't take long to dispatch either. A perfect jelly to end the day on.

Alice cleans off her prize and tucks it into her bag with the others. She wipes her sword on the grass and then gives it a once over with a bit of her blouse, knowing jelly goo on metal leads to rust. Goo on clothes tends to ruin them also, but Alice only ever bought cheap clothes, knowing they wouldn't last her anyway. The young fox catches her breath, sheathing her precious sword on her back, and gazes at the setting sun. She would have to hurry if she wanted to make a supply run today. The Tokala tries to take a drink from her water skin, only to be reminded that it was already empty. With an annoyed grumble, the little fox girl dashes from the edge of the forest to her village.

While Alice did not live in the village, she had once and frequented it enough that she was known by many there. Most of them were aware of her talent for getting rid of the pesky jellies that often crept out of the nearby forest. As such, she had acquired the title 'monster hunter' of which she was very proud. As she blurs past toward the trading post, a few of the villagers smile and wave. She holds her bag tight as she runs, not wanting to lose any of her valuable cargo in the sprint to reach the store before closing. Her lungs burn as she forces more air into them, her throat dry enough to make her tongue stick in places, and her legs ache to the point of wobbling but she makes it. The simple wooden door is still standing open.

"Here she comes, Mom!" Ashleigh calls from the doorway, skipping out to greet the slowing monster hunter.

Ashleigh Graysen was one of very few Alice would call a friend. The Didel, is of an age and height with Alice, kind, and somewhat envious of the other girl's rather venturous lifestyle. The only daughter of the trading post's owner, the widowed Ms. Graysen, she was often expected to stay by the shop, learning the various tasks needed to keep it maintained. She had lost her father in the current war just as Alice had, though she at least still had her mother. Alice had lost both parents, her father to fighting and her mother to the grief after.

The young opossum girl wears a plan sky blue dress over her white patched light gray fur. She is slim but not terribly so, white faced with cute rounded black ears, large aqua marine eyes, and a small pink nose at the end of an angular muzzle. She has an abnormally long, hairless, dark gray tail that tends to drag behind her leaving a trail anywhere she leaves a footprint.

As Alice comes to a stop, panting hard with hands resting on her knees, Ashleigh asks excitedly, as she often did, "How many did you get today?"

Alice briefly holds up seven fingers and Ashleigh bubbles, "That's wonderful! You beat your record!" The Didel has a cup of water held in pink furless fingers and holds it out to the exhausted fox. After a few more breaths, Alice gratefully accepts it. Ashleigh waits patiently, smiling at Alice as she downs the water in one long drink.

Alice hands back the empty cup and wipes her mouth on a sleeve, "Thanks, Ash."

Ashleigh grins widely, taking the cup along with Alice's wrist, "Come on, come on, Mom's waitin'." The Didel then hurriedly leads her into the store.

"Alice," Ms. Graysen greets warmly from behind the counter, goods of various sorts stacked neatly on shelves behind and around her. "How was hunting today? Get some nice cores for me?" Ms. Graysen looks like Ashleigh might in a decade or so, similar in color and shape though her eyes are brown as is her simple dress.

"I got seven," Alice announces with pride, placing her bag atop the counter before the kindly woman.

"Seven? Goodness, you are getting better at dealing with those monsters for us," Ms. Graysen says, impressed.

"It's a new record, Momma!" Ashleigh adds excitedly, peering into the bag. She always liked to see Alice's haul.

Ms. Graysen pulls out one of the orbs for inspection, "Mmm, some nice ones here too. What can I get you for the bunch?"

"Two loaves of that nut bread and a smoked trout if there's any left please," Alice orders hopefully. She almost always came in from hunts late in the evening after much of Ms. Graysen's choice stock was already gone.

"You're in luck. I made sure to save one just for you when Ashleigh saw you headin' out this mornin'. Figured you'd work up a hunger," the opossum woman says, reaching somewhere under her counter to produce a whole fish wrapped in wide leaves, its tail sticking out of one end. She then grabs two long loaves of bread from a basket on a shelf behind her while Ashleigh collects the core stones.

"Thank you, ma'am," the young fox returns with a wide smile, putting her purchases into her shoulder bag, the bread half poking out under her slender arm.

The mother opossum picks up the smallest core stone, "Looks like you still have some left over. You wanna spend it now or put it to the debt?"

"I'll put anything left over to the debt, ma'am," Alice replies, adjusting her sword and bag straps.

After the news of Alice's father's death reached home, her mother gave in to a horrible grief. It took her slowly. At times, Alice would find her in the middle of a chore and just start to cry inconsolably, while other times she would have trouble getting out of bed. As it got worse, she couldn't work and wouldn't eat. Even the cries of her terrified kit couldn't rouse her to any action. Eventually, she withered away, leaving Alice alone. During this time she had worked up a debt which passed to the young Tokala. Without the money to pay it, her home was taken and she was left on the street. Even then there was still some left over, mostly owed to the Didel shopkeeper for having provided for them when they couldn't manage.

Alice had kept the sword left by her father, the only thing she had to remember him by. She had heard from her mother that he was a great swordsman and had finally felt Alice was old enough to learn when he and all the other men, even the able boys, were called to war. Very few had yet returned and they only because of grievous and often crippling wounds. With the men gone, the women, younger boys, and girls had to take on the additional work loads. The labor shortage meant limited supplies and increased prices, which tightened everyone's belts.

Some good did come of it though. The men generally cut back the unusually fast growing nearby forest every now and again, keeping plenty of space between the village and the monster filled woods. Now, with no one to do the work, the forest steadily grew closer as did the threat of monster attacks. It took time but Alice eventually got the courage to face the jellies, the least dangerous but most commonly encountered of the monsters. In doing so, she began to fill an important niche as the local monster hunter.

Ashleigh clasps her hands and begs her mother, "Can I go walk with Alice, please?"

Ms. Graysen purses her lips to the smaller opossum, "Alright, but be back before sundown, and don't leave the village."

Ashleigh gives a little cheer and Alice smiles, "Thanks, Ms. Graysen," she says as she prepares to depart.

"You got it, hon, keep safe out there!" the opossum woman calls as Alice heads out the door, Ashleigh following close behind.

The moment the girls step out, Ashleigh bubbles, "Seven in one day! You're so amazing Alice. I wish I could go on hunts too. Remember when you brought in your first one?" Alice smiles and nods, letting her friend get out all her pent up conversation. "You were so proud when you showed it to Mom, covered in jelly and mud from head to toe," she giggles. Alice remembers that time well. Being alone, it was terrifying. She survived with the help of some of the kinder people in the village, Ashleigh's mother included. But times were tough and no one could afford to give much.

Alice recalls that it was raining a lot then. The jellies tended to dry out if caught in too much sun, so they rarely left the forest. The rains, though, made the days dark and wet, perfect for the slow monsters to venture forth. Alice's first encounter with one had been by complete surprise. She had seen her father dispatching jellies with ease when he was alive and knew how it was to be done, but she quickly discovered that knowing and doing were two very different things.

It was particularly cloudy that day, even at noon. It had rained all night and finally stopped in the morning. Alice was allowed a bed at a villager's house that had lost a son in the war. The grieving mother couldn't afford to feed her so Alice was wandering about in the wide fields between the village and the forest, listening to her stomach growling. She had been eating edible plants she could find, wild spinach and dandelions mostly, but desperately needed something more filling. As she walked, eyes searching the ground, she came across a small green jelly.

Alice was frightened at first. She had her sword true, but had rarely swung it. Up to that point, it was mostly a heavy weight on her back that reminded her off all she had lost. As she watched the jelly, slowly making its way, seemingly oblivious of her, the young Tokala's fear steadily turned to curiosity. She watched it for a long while as it moved along, somewhat like a slug, a trail of discolored grass in its wake. She dropped a few bits of fresh grass atop it and watched as it absorbed them, the grass slowly losing its color and form as it drifted through the viscous ooze until it too was left, yellowed in its trail. Alice had tried shouting at it and tossing rocks, but it didn't seem interested in either. She finally decided to draw her sword, heavy and cumbersome in her untried hands.

Alice first tried an overhead swing but missed, the blow kicking up grass and mud. She tried several more times, and finally managed to hit the edge of her slow moving target. The jelly simply kept moving along, the ooze of its body shifting around the blade and reforming, leaving a goo filled slit, but even that disappeared moments later. Alice was not deterred by her waning strength or the jelly's apparent imperviousness. She continued to side step along with the creature, flailing away at it until its tiny core stone, no bigger than her finger tip, was left in a puddle of ooze. She bought her first meal that day.

Ashleigh talks on about how boring it is running a store and how fun and free it must be to go out hunting monsters, while Alice reminds her of the pros of having a safe life dealing with civilized people. It was a conversation they had often. Ashleigh had a much romanticized view of what her fox friend did; bravely saving the town, living without walls, and exploring the wild forest. While Alice did occasionally rid the village of a stray jelly or two, had no walls in which to live, and led expeditions into the forest when she could afford it, she also had to make an exhaustingly simple living, fighting almost every day just to have enough to eat.

The young hunter was improving all the time, but things were not all heroism and fun. Jellies, while not overly dangerous, could be troublesome if not treated carefully. Often while hunting, Alice would end up with globs of corrosive goop on her bare fur, and if she didn't have enough water to wash it off within a time, it could lead to a horribly itchy rash that might last hours or even days. This tended to happen mostly on her feet, hands, and sometimes ears. A major rash on the feet might keep her off them, which meant no cores and no food. Even now there were times when she had to choose between enduring the, sometimes intense, irritation or going hungry. Fighting monsters on an empty stomach was no easy task.

The two girls reach the village's well and Ashleigh turns the crank to bring up the water bucket. She often did, something the tired young fox was always grateful for, all while talking about going on a hunt with her, maybe, at some point, in the future. This was also something Ashleigh did often. She'd go on about various preparations she'd make, how long they could stay out, and how many jellies she'd like to find. But the Didel would always shoot her plans down, knowing her mother would never let her do something so dangerous. Alice found it fun talking to Ashleigh about hunts. It gave her someone to bounce ideas off of and it made her happy to share her knowledge of jellies.

The girls talk as Alice fills her two small water skins. In her experience, it never hurt to have extra water. She drinks most of one to refresh herself and fills it again. "Maybe if I had a weapon, Mom would let me come with you," Ashleigh considers allowed, "What do you think would work?" The small village had no blacksmiths and Alice's sword was a rarity.

"A good club might do it. Jellies aren't terribly tough, and if you hit hard enough, you could probably knock enough jelly away to get the core," the young fox suggests, putting the straps of her water skins over her neck and then adds, "I can try to find you a stout branch in the woods next time I'm out."

Ashleigh claps her hands, "Oh, would you? That would be wonderful! Then we could fight monster together!" The young opossum takes a few swings with a phantom club.

The sun is dropping over the horizon making everything cast long shadows and Alice parts from her friend with a hug. "Be careful, Alice!" Ashleigh waves before turning back toward her mother's shop while the monster hunter heads out into the fields.

Just as dusk settles in, she makes it to her own home, a small tent atop a grassy hill in the shadow of a large oak tree. Its summer now and there won't be any need to start a fire in the ring of stones she had set up just for such a purpose. The fox unloads her gear and sits with her back against the great tree's trunk with a water skin and her leaf wrapped trout.

This was a rare treat that Alice only allowed after an exceptional hunt. "Beating my record counts I think," she says aloud, unwrapping her feast. She takes in a deep inhale through the nostrils, letting the smoky aroma fill her lungs. As if on cue, her stomach burbles and she digs in. While Alice has her supper, she looks to the forest some ways off and sees no jellies. The Tokala had chosen this spot for her camp for several reasons, the main being that it gave her a nice view of all the land around her. Jellies tended to slip out from the forest at night when it was cooler and their silent pace meant an unwary hunter might wake up with one in her bed. She hadn't had that problem since she'd saved enough for the tent, but had had it enough to be habitually watchful of activity just before she went to sleep. It was clear tonight.

Once the young fox has her fish and a bit of bread, she picks her teeth for a while with one of the fish's slender bones. She thinks of many things, but tries to focus on one. With the extra bread she'd bought, she finally had enough to make another expedition into the forest, even if only a short one. Alice had always wondered where the jellies kept coming from. It seemed no matter how many she vanquished, more would always appear. As she had started collecting enough of the core stones to merit extra supplies, she had also begun mounting trips deeper into the forest.

Alice learned things on these trips and was eager to go on another. She had discovered how they multiply and, more importantly, she had discovered that there were different colored jellies. While green was the most common, she had seen various shades of brown, yellow, blue, and even red. The reds were very rare and thus their cores could be traded for more. She had slain one, the only she'd ever seen, which is how she managed to afford her tent. But the less common colors were also a prize worth fighting for.

The jellies of different colors did not seem different in any other way, still ponderously slow and indifferent to outside stimuli. Alice had considered the reasons for the different colors many a night and thought it might have something to do with what they ate. The green ones often seemed to have dissolved a lot of grass,the browns, perhaps some wood. Alice could only guess the others managed to slide through some flowers to get their hues. The red one though. Alice had never seen red flowers in the forest or otherwise.

After some thought, the tired hunter yawns and decides it's time to get some sleep. Real dark was nearly upon her but keen vision and a full moon makes it a simple matter to gather her meager belongings and to pack them, along with herself, into her small beige tent. Pushing all her gear off to one side, the little fox stretches, yawns once more, and falls asleep on a pillow of relatively clean clothes. But it doesn't last.

A fast storm blows in during the night bringing with it several powerful crashes of thunder. Alice is jolted awake by the first and simply has to endure the rest. The cleverly made tent keeps the weather out for the most part, but as rain dampens the ground, the cloth floor of the tent cools and moistens too. It's very late when the last of the terrible cracking thunderclaps stops and Alice can finally get to sleep, and when she does, she dreams.

She sees her father, brandishing her sword at formless shadow creatures that encircle him. He swings the weapon into them only to have it pass through harmlessly. The shadows bring him down and begin dragging him away. He drops the sword and claws at the ground as Alice runs after him screaming soundlessly for her father. She takes a second to retrieve the weapon but it tugs at her arm as if too heavy to lift. She looks to see it's her mother, pulling at her wrist from the floor, weeping as she calls her name, "Alice! Alice!" Looking back, Alice's father is being taken further into the distance, fading from sight. Alice desperately reaches for him, unable to free herself from her mother's grasp, her name ringing in her ears, "Alice! ALICE!" She jolts awake again for what seems far too short a time, still hearing her mother screeching. But it isn't her mother. It's Ashleigh.

The Didel isn't screeching but calling urgently into her tent from outside, "Alice? Are you awake? We need your help."

It is entirely too early for the young fox and her body feels horribly sluggish and sore from the day before. She means to ask what is wrong, but only manages an unintelligible grumble.

"Alice? Jellies are near the village! Can I come in?" Ashleigh asks anxiously.

The little hunter turns herself clockwise without actually rising and reaches lazily to the pull string for the tent's door flap.

After a few tries she gives it a tug and Ashleigh pokes her gray furry head in, "Oh, Alice, you have to get up, they're gettin' closer!" The Didel girl reaches in to shake Alice's shoulder.

Alice's eye lids are heavy and dry but she forces them wider and sees her friend, blurry over her.

"Ok, ok," she groans in mild frustration as she places a hand on the Didel's fluffy cheek, weakly pushing her away. Alice sits up and Ashleigh drapes the shoulder bag over the fox, lifting an arm so it sits at her side.

The young opossum does the same with her sword, placing it on Alice's back and begins pushing her, "Go, go, it's hero time!"

Alice grudgingly gets to her feet and shambles out of her tent. The ground is still wet with the night's rain though the sky has cleared. The sun is just rising and already she spots a few jellies. The creatures wander aimlessly, some drifting in the general direction of the village but Alice knows it's more luck than design.

Ashleigh dashes from behind Alice, heading straight for the small settlement while shouting back and waving, "Come on, come on!"

The sleepy hunter rubs her eyes and starts after her, slowly picking up speed as her body awakens. Soon she's bounding after the opossum, feeling invigorated by the easy access to more jellies, and thus, more supplies. She begins to feel rather confident that once she clears any near the village she can sweep the fields and really cash in.

As the girls near the village, they can hear the irritated cries of a woman. Alice adjusts her course to the sound and finds her first opponent of the day. An angry Leeseran is whacking away at an oncoming dark green jelly with a broom. The jelly ignores it, wobbling with the impacts while slowly moving toward the squirrel woman's garden.

A tiny Leeseran girl looks on from a doorway and cheers at the sight of the young hunter, "Momma look, it's Alice!"

The squirrel woman cries, "Alice, please, before it gets my vegetables!"

Alice draws her sword from the sheath on her back and takes up a position beside the invading jelly, careful not to stand in its path. The woman backs away to watch the hunter make a hard vertical slash, cutting a generous portion from the rear of the jelly. Before it can reform around the blade she pulls the sword away from it horizontally, flinging the gooey slice away and into the dirt road. The slice is almost instantly rounded back out as the jelly shrinks, undeterred. Alice continues to take off pieces of the jelly until it's small enough to reach in and extract the core. Once she pulls it free, the rest of the jelly collapses in on itself, no longer animated.

As she cleans off her prize and sword, the squirrel woman thanks her and tells her to wait while she heads inside her house. The little squirrel girl hops out to Alice cheering, "That was amaz-oh."

She stops, looking around at the bits of green goo. Pinching her nose, she blurts, "It stinks!"

Alice smiles, "Yeah, tell your mom to throw some dirt on the pieces and be careful not to step on 'em." Alice had grown used to the smell but it tended to surprise most. The gooey part of the jellies smelled awful and the moment their thicker outer layer was pierced a stench like swamp water would fill the air.

The mother Leeseran returns, her broom replaced by three cookies. She smiles as she approaches Alice but is then visibly struck by the smell. "Oh, word," she exclaims, waving a hand in the air before handing Alice the treats. "Thank you, dear. We're so lucky to have a girl like you around to deal with these, things," she says flittering her fingers at the gooey remains of the jelly.

Alice nods her thanks as the little squirrel bounces up and down, "Momma, Momma. Alice said we had to put dirt on the jelly pieces and we're not supposed to step on them and can I have a cookie?"

"Did you just slay an evil monster?" the mother asks, raising an eyebrow to her daughter. The little squirrel frowns and stops her bouncing, but brightens back up as Alice hands her one of hers. Just as the girl tries to take a bite, her mother lifts a finger, "Ah, what do we say when someone gives us something?"

"Thank you, Alice!" the girl says dutifully and begins gobbling down her snack.

As Alice turns to look for more jellies, she sees Ashleigh grinning widely at her and gives her a cookie too. The opossum thanks her and takes a bite. Alice does as well finding the cookie to be crunchy with nuts and sweet with honey. But before she can finish it a young brown furred Murin boy calls for her, "Alice! Alice! We got a jelly, come quick!" The hunter gives Ashleigh a look and they both cram their cookies into their mouths picking up their pace to follow after the mouse boy.

He leads the two girls to the small communal orchard, a key source of food for the villagers. Several other children and concerned women look on as a rather large, lime green jelly absorbs apples from a basket lying on its side. As far as Alice was aware, jellies could not climb trees, so the apples among the branches were safe, but, if fallen apples kept a jelly around too long, it could damage the trunk and any surface roots it lingered over. As she nears the orchard, she shouts for everyone to get back, brandishing her sword in both hands. The jelly had already taken several apples and they float around near the bottom of it, just starting to decay. Alice kicks the basket away and steps to its side, as she had done before, but makes horizontal slashes to spare any of the nearby tree's precious roots. She had learned early on that horizontal slashes were only effective if she held the blade at an angle so as to cut and remove bits of goo. Any of the syrupy gunk left on or near the jelly would reform into it. The small gathering of people step further away as green slime begins to fly.

After an exhausting bit of work, Alice is left with a nice sized lime green core stone and a few haphazardly sliced bits of browning fruit. The kids cheer and the adults share their thanks along with a few freshly picked apples.

"Wow, that was great! You were like, 'Get back!' And then woosh woosh woosh!" Ashleigh exclaims, swinging an imaginary sword as the girls step out into the fields to share the fruit. Alice grins and flops on the ground trying to catch her breath while cleaning off her weapon.

"Well, well, Ms. Dippleblack, you've managed to save the village once more."

The girls look over to Ms. Graysen making her way to them.

"Mom! Did you see? Wasn't Alice amazing?" Ashleigh bubbles.

"She certainly was," the older opossum agrees and then hands a new white blouse to Alice, "Here child, we can't have our hero walkin' around in rags."

Alice looks over herself, her blouse torn in places and covered with stains, old and new, and then gratefully accepts the blouse with a smile, "Thanks, Ms. Graysen."

"Mm-hm," the mother opossum nods and then tells her daughter, "Ashleigh, I could use your help at the store."

"Oh, Mom, but I'm helping Alice with the jellies," Ashleigh whines.

"I'm sure she can manage, and *you* have your own job to do," counters Ms. Graysen.

"Ugh, fine," the young Didel groans and then waves as she follows her mother, "Bye Alice, I'll see you later, right?"

Alice waves back, "Yeah, I'll probably stop in this evening!"

As the young Tokala watches the pair leave, a sudden pang of loneliness grips her heart. Before the old foe could strengthen its hold, she shoves it away and gets to her feet, refocusing on her quest. Trails of yellowed grass make the remaining jellies easy to find in the fields. Two have progressed toward the village but were still a ways off. It was nearing noon now and the sun seemed to slow the monsters even more. Alice dispatches them easily despite her waning stamina. She follows a third trail for a time, bringing down its maker before deciding she is done for the day.

Bagging the five cores, the young hunter heads for the stream. It was a popular spot for fishing, cleaning, and bathing due to its proximity to the village. Alice, finding the coast to be clear, slips out of her dirty goo covered clothes and wades in. She gets just deep enough to be able to submerge herself in the cool, slow moving water while seated on the rocky bottom. She does what she can to wash the goo off her blouse, but knows it'll only be good as rags and bedding now. Her sturdier pants, however, will survive a few more battles.

Alice carefully washes the jelly from her fur, checking and rechecking to be sure she got it all. Toes, ears, back and tail, all get a thorough cleaning. She's going through the later when she hears the sound of a blade chopping into wood. She lowers into the water, only letting her head show, and turns to the shore where she left her belongings. There, Arnold Duncan is trying to pull out her sword from the tree trunk he's managed to lodge it in.

"Hey, get away from my sword!" Alice shouts from the water. The young Urock gives her an annoyed look and then gives the blade's handle a few more tugs. Alice manages to slip on her soaked pants as she shouts again, "Get away from it, NOW!"

Arnold gives up on his efforts and turns to face Alice. If he were green, Arnold Duncan would look very much like a hairy pear. The bear boy's small head and rather bulbous body were instead covered in brown fur. He wears a yellow shirt that struggles valiantly but fails to cover his round stomach and equally straining gray pants. His beady, black eyes glare at Alice as he lumbers to the shore line, but before his feet reach the water he growls, "Or what? You can't do nothin' without that sword."

Like most of the village's children, Arnold's father was taken by the war. The boy was too young at the time to be conscripted and without a father's discipline the years since had turned him into a bully. The Urock people were large by nature and Arnold was no exception. Perhaps two years younger than Alice, he still managed to outgrow her by a considerable sum in both height and weight. Alice, however, knew that much of the time he got by on his size alone and hadn't yet learned to wield his strength to any great effect. But Alice knew her strength. She was smaller but faster.

After some quick calculation, Alice makes her move. Covering her modest chest with one forearm, she makes a splashy sprint for the boy, who raises one clawed hand back to strike. On her approach, Alice hurls her soaked blouse into Arnold's snarling face. In the seconds it takes him to wipe the wet garment away, she hefts a fist size rock from the river bed and brings it down on the boy's hairy foot with as much force as both her slender arms can muster. The boy howls in pain and immediately tries to grasp the aching appendage over his girth but loses his balance and falls over.

The fox girl darts to her bag and slips into her new blouse, doing just a few buttons, as the large boy rolls around crying. She then pushes rather than pulls her sword free and brings the tip to Arnold's throat. She waits a moment to let the situation register through the density of the boy's skull and then speaks as evenly as she can manage, "If you ever touch my things again, I'm gonna to skin you alive and leave you naked in the woods for the monsters." She then makes a show of looking over him, adding, "I've always wanted a bear skin coat." Arnold quivers, his eyes glued to the sword's point as a moist spot appears and expands rapidly over his pants. Alice grins, "Don't go ruinin' *my* coat." With that she gathers her things and heads back to her camp, leaving the boy in his puddle.

At her tent, Alice hangs her damp trousers and blouse on a line of string to dry while pulling on another pair. These are blue and a bit bigger so she needs to tie a bit of rope at her waist to keep them over her slender hips. She then plops down to check her sword for any damage, sighing when she finds a chip in the edge. It's one of several but this one is definitely new. She gets her sharpening stone and tries to straighten out the area around it the best she can. Alice tires quickly, the lack of sleep, battles with jellies, and annoying bears sapping her limited reserves of stamina, but she is determined to finish her precious work.

Once Alice is satisfied, she replaces her prized possession in its sheath before falling to her back, arms spread at her sides. She wants nothing more than to take a nap, but the sun is already starting to set and if she wants to make any trades with her new cores, she would have to leave now. The tired Tokala grumbles as she places her sword over her head on one shoulder so it hangs diagonally down her back, gathers her bag of precious cores, and heads back to the village for the second time in one day.

She's made good time and is nearly to Ms. Graysen's store when a gruff female voice bellows, "Alice Dippleblack! How *dare* you threaten my cub!"

Alice jumps and turns to see a massive figure looming over her. Arnold's mother is nearly as wide as she is tall and Alice has to pan her gaze upward just to take her in. Very similar in appearance to her horrible child, though with a darker color to her fur, Ms. Duncan towers over the young fox girl. Glaring with her beady black eyes and baring a mouth full of sharp teeth, the large woman looks terribly fierce from Alice's low vantage point.

"You will apologize to him right now!" she roars pointing back to her plump son.

Arnold grins absurdly from behind his imposing mother despite not having yet changed his pants.

Alice, perhaps too tired to consider that with one swipe, Ms. Duncan could end her days as a hunter, or simply being at a stubborn age, begins in a voice she feels sounds very grown up, "Arnold stole and damaged my sword while I was bathing in the stream."

"She lyin', Momma!" Arnold shouts in defense, pointing a fat accusing finger at Alice.

"He told me you attacked him with that weapon and said you'd skin him and wear him as a coat!" Ms. Duncan growls back.

Keeping as composed as she can manage, Alice continues, "Then I'm sorry that he's a liar, a bully..." she then cranes her neck around to glare at Arnold, "and a coward."

The bear woman roars her anger and advances on Alice, snarling ferociously, "I've always said you were too young to have such a dangerous weapon. Now you've threatened my cub, MY CUB! You will give it here right-"

"Ms. Duncan, *that* is *enough!*" Ms. Graysen shouts from her store doorway just behind Alice. The opossum woman steps out and puts a hand on Alice's shoulder while looking the large Urock in the eye, "It is a known fact that your cub has become quite the trouble maker of late. As such, I tend to believe Alice when she says your boy was the one who instigated whatever happened between them."

Ms. Graysen stands her ground even when Ms. Duncan growls, "How dare you say such things about my cub. He is a paragon!"

"Hardly," the Didel shoots back, "My Ashleigh says he's grown rather fond of pulling and stepping on her tail."

Other parents, attracted by the commotion, reveal similar grievances including hitting, pushing, and scratching, all perpetrated by Arnold.

Reinforced by the other villagers, Ms. Graysen threatens, "If you don't get your boy in check, you'll have to find somewhere else to buy your ham and fish."

The Urock mother huffs several times and looks ready to explode, but instead snorts angrily and turns, grabbing Arnold by the arm to drag him away. Once they've gone off, Ms. Graysen lets out a breath and seems to shrink a little, her long, bare gray tail dropping to the ground from where it had lifted behind her.

Alice finally lets herself shiver, fear, anger, and adrenaline taking their tolls as she looks up to the woman, "Thanks, Ms. Graysen."

The opossum woman gives her a small smile as Ashleigh comes up beside her, "Phew, that was tense."

"Hush child," her mother chides as she kneels and turns Alice toward her, both hands on the fox girl's shoulders, "Now Alice, you should know better than to antagonize that woman."

"But Arnold stole my sword and even chipped it," she whines, a tear threatening to emerge but Ms. Graysen interrupts.

"I have no doubts he did. That boy's been a problem for a while now. But I have to tell you, if Ms. Duncan lost anymore of her temper," she takes in a breath and looks after the lumbering Urocks, "I don't think the village together could have stopped her from tearing you apart."

Alice looks at the bear pair too and sniffs, "I'm sorry, Ms. Graysen."

The opossum woman gives the Tokala a hug, "It's alright, all's well now." Ashleigh joins in, squeezing her muzzle in between her friend and her mother, making them both smile.

"I have some more cores to trade if you're still open," Alice announces proudly.

In Ms. Graysen's store, Alice trades her five jelly core stones for more bread, she was awfully tempted to get another trout but decided to purchase a greater quantity of the cheaper food.

Just as Alice is accepting her goods from the matronly opossum, Ashleigh bursts, "Did you really say you were gonna skin Arnold and wear him like a coat?"

Alice grins, "Maybe."

The Didel girl laughs. "You're so brave, Alice. I wish I could tell 'im off like that. Oh, that boy is just terrible."

Alice agrees, placing the bread into her shoulder bag.

Ashleigh asks, "What'd you buy all that bread for? You know it'll probably go stale before you can eat it," then she sucks in a breath, "Are you going on another one of your expeditions?"

"Yup, I'm headin' out tomorrow morning. This should last me a couple o' days," Alice replies happily.

Ashleigh bobs on her feet, "Oh that sounds so excitin', I'd love to come with you-"

"But you have chores to do right here," her mother finishes for her from behind the counter.

Ashleigh frowns, settling down and then asks, "Mom, can I go with Alice to the well?"

"Not this time, dear, I need your help closin'," the Didel woman returns as she hurries about, placing displayed items back into containers for the night.

"Awww," the young opossum moans and leans in to whisper to Alice, "If you can, try to find me a good clubbin' stick."

"I'll try," Alice whispers back.

Ashleigh grins and says in her normal tone of voice, "Bye and take care. I want you to tell me all about it when you get back."

"Be careful, Alice. If things get too dangerous you come right back, you hear?" her mother adds.

The Tokala hikes up her shoulder bag and calls back to both, "I will!" and then heads out the door.

After filling her water skins at the well, Alice heads back to camp. She has the rest of her first loaf of bread for dinner, settles into her tent, and immediately falls asleep.

Chapter 2

A Trio

The following morning Alice wakes up late but well rested. The young fox stretches, looking forward to the new day and her first expedition in weeks. She has a simple breakfast of bread and water while gathering all she needs for the trip, draping all four of her water skins over her neck. The forest has water sources she knows but they were a popular spot for monsters and ferals, making them sometimes difficult to reach. Along with all her bread, she also takes her rag pants and blouse, a bit of rope, and of course, her sword. Emerging from her tent, she judges by the sun that it's nearly noon, a little later than she'd planned but the day is bright and perfect for exploring.

Crossing the fields to the forest's edge, Alice sees no jelly activity, a good sign. She often spent her days just on the edge where the forest and field meet, keeping any jellies from crossing over. It was rare that they did, especially when it hadn't rained. Jellies dry out if left in the sun too long. Several times she'd come across cracked and broken cores from those that have, the goo housing them having evaporated, leaving the stones frail, brittle, and worthless. The jellies fascinated Alice greatly, not only because they were a source of income but because she believed they were magical in origin.

As she steps into the shade of the thick forest canopy, the intrepid hunter finds the small path she'd taken before and heads in. After trekking for only a few minutes, it feels like she's entered another world. The forest is a place of wild things, complete with new sights, sounds, and smells. It's also cooler here, the moist air adding to the mystique. Thick undergrowth limits vision in all directions and the cries her pointed fox ears pick up are proof that there are more than jellies among the trees, plenty more. Still, she presses on with determination and purpose.

After near an hour's march through the dense forest, she reaches the site of her previous camp. From here she had led short ventures out deeper in but would always come back to this spot. This time though, the small clearing was taken over by local flora. The various shrubs and even trees of the forest seemed to grow faster than those outside it. She cuts through a few large leafed plants with her sword to find that the small pool, the primary reason for choosing this spot, has dried up. The recent rain had moved too fast to leave even a puddle. A little disappointed but not deterred, Alice takes a break to down some water and then sets off in search of a new camp site.

Keeping her heading as best she can by tracking the sun in the few places she can see it, Alice travels in what she is fairly sure is a western direction. She avoids the few jellies she sees in an effort to save her strength for after the establishment of her camp. Other creatures are about as well, lizards, frogs, squirrels, spiders, and other things that flee at the sound of her steps, going unseen. She had often been told that ferals, animals that can't walk on two legs or talk, can be dangerous, but in Alice's experience, the smaller ones at least are of little threat. Still, she avoids any spider webs she sees and is constantly scanning the ground for anything she would rather not step on.

By late afternoon, she comes across a small brook falling down in steps over some rocks. Nothing immediately dangerous present, Alice settles on the ground, lying down her gear to snacks on some of her bread. She drinks her fill from her skins and as she tops them off, her eyes catch sight of something rather unusual. Climbing over a fallen tree's trunk, some feet away, is an extraordinarily large caterpillar. Its body is as thick as her fist and about twice as long as her finger. But what really makes it stand out is its bright green color. She decides to rest and watch the fat bug make its slow, undulating way across the dead tree.

This was hardly the first caterpillar Alice had seen, but it was the first to be so large. She glances around to see if there are more but this is the only one that stands out. She watches for a while, catching her breath and giving her legs a break. It has a series of black dots along its side and pink spots surrounding each. She continues to watch when its hind legs hold its front up as it decides to climb up a tree and then in a flash of movement, disappears.

Alice jumps, looking ahead of where the bug vanished to find at first what appears to be a very large lizard. Its body is greatly obstructed by a leafy branch but the lizard's mouth opening a few times as it swallows the unfortunate caterpillar is unmistakable. Then it looks at Alice. After a brief pause, she scoots back on her rump to get in reaching distance of her sword before the lizard speaks.

"Hope you weren't planning to eat that," it says in a non-threatening female voice. The lizard then crawls down the tree's trunk to the forest floor and stands on its hind legs.

"You… you're not a feral?" Alice asks in surprise.

"Do I look like one?" the lizard girl asks, waving her hands over herself and giving a little spin.

Alice takes a moment to look over the unusual stranger. Even slouching, she is taller than Alice but not by much. Her skin is patterned in browns that blend in well with the surrounding trees, though her eyes, by contrast, are a vibrant green. She has no fur anywhere and wears what looks like animal hides for clothing, though they're rather dirty and in need of repair. The torn leather reveals that her lighter brown countershading starting on her lower jaw reaches from her neck, over her belly, and down her inner thighs, stopping above her knees. The lizard girl has a tapering rounded muzzle with two small nostril slits near the end. Her limbs are long and lean with dark gray to nearly black claws on her fingers and large curved talons on her feet. Behind her drags a tail at least twice as long as her legs. It starts very thick at her rump and tapers to a rounded point no wider than Alice's pinkie.

"Enjoying yourself?" the strange girl asks, tilting her head slightly to one side and drawing Alice's gaze back to her face.

"Wha-What? Who are you?" the Tokala stammers, having never seen such a being before.

The lizard girl smirks, "I'm Danahlia, but most just call me Danny," then with a nod she says, "Your turn."

Not wanting to seem weak or frightened, Alice stands up, "I'm Alice, Alice Dippleblack."

"Dippleblack?" Danahlia grins, "That's kinda cute. I get it, with the hands and the feet, and your ears," she says sticking up clawed fingers on either side of her head to mimic Alice's ears. The lizard girl has none, only two small holes low on the sides of her head. Alice gawks at her uncertainly, prompting the stranger to continue, "And what are you doing in these dangerous woods all alone, Alice Dippleblack?"

For some reason, Alice did not care for the way the girl had said her name. This makes her reach down and place her sword sling over her shoulder, not to threaten but to show it was there before replying, "I'm a monster hunter."

Danahlia places a considering finger to the side of her mouth, "Is that right?"

Alice doesn't reply and begins loading up her water skins and shoulder bag full of bread while keeping an eye on the strange girl.

Once she has her things she finds Danahlia looking at her, smiling pleasantly with her hands behind her back, "Well, monster hunter, Alice Dippleblack, it is very nice to meet you. I like your tail."

Alice raises a brow, a bit put off by her candor, "Thanks."

The lizard girl takes a few steps closer and leans forward as if to peek around the fox, "Can I, touch it?"

Just to keep on even terms, and not at all because she's curious herself, Alice answers, "Only if I can touch yours."

Danahlia's smile brightens and she steps closer, her lengthy tail curling around and rising to Alice's side. As Alice reaches out and touches the long appendage, Danahlia steps around her other side to do the same with hers. A Tokala's tail is rather sensitive but Danahlia's touch is very gentle and reassuringly slow. Alice finds the contact to be rather nice though she had no intention of admitting it. Alice, in turn, runs her fingers down the lizard girl's tapered tail to find it very smooth and surprisingly firm.

Danahlia takes hold of Alice's tail loosely but close enough to the base to make her twitch before running her fingers in a loop down to the tip. As she fiddles with the white fur there, she gushes, "I love your tail, it's so..." she searches for a word, "...poofy!"

Alice gives a half grin, "Thanks, yours is really nice too, it's, so long."

Danahlia makes a pleased, "Mmm," and her tail drifts away from Alice's reach as she stands before her, "Well, now that we're friends, there's someone else I'd like you to meet."

The words alert the young fox and she scans the surrounding area, taking a step back.

The lizard girl laughs, "Calm down. Ticks, you're a jumpy one. Don't worry, she's a Warm Blood like you."

Danahlia starts off deeper into the forest as Alice looks on. Alice had never met anyone in the forest before nor had she ever encountered one of Danahlia's lizard kin. She found this all very suspicious but also immensely fascinating.

Torn between caution and curiosity, she ends up simply standing still until Danahlia comes back and waves a hand for her to follow, "Come on, Alice Dippleblack, she's just over here." Tipping the scales over to curiosity, the fox girl follows.

Passing by a tree, the larger girl picks up a stick that looks like she may have been trying to fashion it into a spear.

She uses it now as a walking aid. "So, Alice Dippleblack," she chortles, "I like your name," and then more conversationally continues, "What monsters do you hunt out here with that sword o' yours?"

Alice, still scanning her surroundings as if to spot an ambush, replies, "Jellies mostly."

"Jellies? You mean those roundish clearish blobbish things that eat everything they touch?" Danahlia asks in surprise, turning to her.

Alice stops, instinctively putting a hand on the handle of her sword, "Yeah."

Danahlia cocks her head to one side, "You can kill them?"

"Yeah," Alice says again but then considers. In truth, she had never thought of herself as killing them. After all, jellies never really seemed alive to begin with. Without mouths, eyes, ears, or any organs they just seemed like things. Things that moved sure, but not like living things. They raised no young, did not communicate in any way, and didn't even seem to have a sense of self preservation. They just consumed things around them and multiplied.

Danahlia ignores her cautious stance and goes on asking, "How? I've stabbed 'em but they don't die, or even really bleed."

The thought of having someone to share her knowledge of the jellies relaxes the young fox girl a little and she replies, "You have to remove their core stones."

"Core stones? Those things that float around inside 'em?" Danahlia inquires curiously as she resumes walking.

"Yup, they're valuable, you know?" Alice returns, following along.

"Really? I thought those had something to do with it, but the last one I tried to reach into made my hand burn."

Alice grins at the amateur mistake, "Yeah, if you can, you want to avoid getting too much jelly on you. The best way to deal with 'em is to get rid of as much o' the main body as you can before nabbin' it."

"How do you do that? Oh, wait, Twinkie's gonna wanna hear this," Danahlia says, leading Alice to a small clearing and calling out, "Hey, Twinkie, look what I found!"

A small girl's voice groans, "I am rather sure I've already informed you that I do not like being addressed as, Twinkie."

Alice homes in on the voice to find a robed figure emerging from behind some rocks. Alice knew that she was somewhat small for her age, but if she was small, this girl is tiny. And she soon sees why. As the girl shows herself, she pulls back the hood of her robe to reveal that she is a Murin, one of the diminutive mouse people.

Danahlia gives the little mouse a negligent wave of her hand, "Oh sure you do. Anyway, this is Alice Dippleblack. She knows how to kill those goopy things. Even says there's money in it," the lizard girl explains, wrapping her tail about Alice's waist to bring her close enough to put a companionable hand on her shoulder. "Alice, this is-"

"Twinkaleni Orbear," the mouse girl interrupts, giving Alice a slight bow before looking up at her.

Alice had seen Murin before but this one was small even by their standards. She did, however, possess the largest ears she had ever seen on any of them. Twinkaleni's ears are circular in shape and both nearly as large as her head. Standing, the mouse girl could just come up to Alice's waist if her great ears were included. She has light gray fur with a lighter, near white, counter shading. Twinkaleni has inquisitive amber eyes and a tiny pink nose that sniffs the air between them. The rest of her small form is covered by a tattered but functional brown robe. Even so, little pink toes can be seen protruding from under it.

Seeing the cute little mouse girl erases all suspicion and Alice walks over to Twinkaleni, dropping to her knees, "Oh cheese! You are so adorable!"

She is on the verge of grabbing the little mouse girl up in her arms but Twinkaleni recoils uncomfortably, "Yes, well, thank you."

Danahlia chortles from behind, "She doesn't like to be touched much."

Alice's arms hang in the air and she's tempted to hug the cute mouse anyway, eager to feel what looks to be very fine fur in her fingers, but then drops them, not wanting to be rude.

The tiny mouse relaxes, "It is nice to meet you, Alice. Do you live locally?"

Alice is transfixed by the girl's expansive ears, her fingers rubbing together unconsciously, "Uh, yeah, near Toki. It's a village just east o' here." Twinkaleni watches Alice's hands cautiously as the fox asks, "What about you guys?"

Twinkaleni opens her mouth but Danahlia answers, "We just got here, place looked like a nice spot to find some grub."

"Do you live nearby? In another village?" the inquisitive fox wonders, standing back up.

Again Twinkaleni opens her mouth but Danahlia answers first, "We don't really *live* anywhere. We go where it's safe, or safe-ish. But we were runnin' low on supplies so we decided to check in here."

"You can trade for food and things at my village. I can take you there," Alice says helpfully, looking to the lizard girl.

"Oh, uh, we don't really have any money... or stuff," Danahlia replies her eyes dropping to the ground.

"Yes, yes, but you mentioned you can slay those gelatinous," Twinkaleni starts but sniffs the air some more before finishing, "blobs?"

Alice looks to her curiously, "The jellies? Yeah."

"And that doing so is profitable?" Twinkaleni asks, still sniffing, her cute little pink nose angling around to Alice's shoulder bag.

"Oh sure, if you collect the cores you can exchange them at the trade post."

"Wonderful. By chance is that bread I smell? I'm sorry to intrude but I'm dreadfully hungry. The only thing we've had to eat since we've arrived are, bugs," Twinkaleni says distastefully.

"I like bugs," Danahlia comments merrily as Alice grabs one of the loaves of bread she had been working on and hands it to the mouse girl.

Twinkaleni accepts it graciously, "Oh, thank you. I'm afraid I don't share my companion's fondness for insects." She immediately begins eating, revealing a set of small incisors that only add to her appeal.

"Don't mention it," Alice smiles, glad to be able to help her new friends.

As Twinkaleni munches ravenously, Danahlia asks, "So how do you get to those core thingies without touchin' 'em?"

"I use my sword to cut away at 'em. The more jelly you remove, the smaller they get, until you can just reach in and grab 'em," Alice explains, swinging a phantom sword. "But it does take a bit of effort," she adds looking to the rather fragile looking Murin.

Danahlia grins, "Don't worry about Twinkie, she's a mage."

Alice lifts a brow, "What does that mean, mage?"

"Means she can use magic!" the lizard girl exclaims, gesturing grandly with both arms.

"Magic? Really?" Alice asks skeptically. She had heard of witches and wizards in stories but had never known, or even known anyone who had known, someone who could use magic.

Twinkaleni's eyes have gone wide, crumbs dropping from her mouth as Danahlia grins, "Yeah, better show her, Twinkie."

"Duhna!" Twinkaleni shouts harshly through a mouthful of bread.

"What? Oh, yeah. Uh, I think we can trust her. Right?" Danahlia directs the last to Alice.

The Tokala tilts her head curiously, "Sure, you can trust me."

The mouse girl gives her companion an irritated look and then shakes her head, swallowing. She tucks the rest of her bread somewhere into her robe with a huff, "Very well. Look closely now, Alice." She extends her loosely sleeved arms before her and upward with both tiny pink palms held as if pushing on an invisible wall. She then calls out, "Vespis flowmino!"

Alice looks to where her hands are aimed to see the leaves on a branch there begin to move as if in a light breeze, though she feels none present. Alice's eyes widen in anticipation as the breeze strengthens a little, but then dies down.

She looks around in the general area fearing she had missed it, just as Twinkaleni huffs, "There... did you see that? Got most of the leaves... to move that time."

Alice raises a brow, "Was that it? I can do that." She then draws her sword and taps the same branch with the tip, making it shake with equal if not greater force than Twinkaleni's spell.

Danahlia barks a laugh, "Ha! She's got you there, Twinkie."

The little mouse girl narrows her eyes at both of them, "Yes, well, clearly I am weary from travel and hunger. You watch. Once I have my full strength back, I will amaze even you." She then retrieves her bread to resume eating.

Fascinated, if slightly less impressed than she had planned to be, Alice asks, "Can you show me how to use magic?"

With her cheeks full, Twinkaleni extends Alice a hand and motions for the Tokala to give her hers. Alice does so, placing a few fingers on Twinkaleni's tiny pink palm.

Immediately the mouse shakes her head in the negative and then swallows, "I'm sorry, Alice. I don't believe you have the proper aptitude to use magic."

The fox girl looks at her hand up close, seeing nothing at all wrong with it, "How can you tell?"

Before she can take another bite, Twinkaleni replies, "When two magically gifted individuals touch, they can feel the energy of the other's aura. It's sort of like a slow static shock. I didn't get it from you and it didn't look like you felt mine."

Alice frowns at the news and Danahlia puts a comforting hand on her shoulder, "Don't pant it. Twinkie says I can't use magic either. Apparently, it's pretty rare."

Alice waves her blade a little, cheering herself up, "Well, at least I have this."

The lizard girl smiles and claps her hand on her shoulder lightly just as Twinkaleni is finishing off her bread.

"Indeed, now about those, jellies?" the mouse girl says, putting an upward inflection on the name.

"Yeah, that's what we call 'em around Toki," says Alice, sheathing her weapon.

Twinkaleni opens her mouth to say something but Danahlia beats her to it, "What are they?"

"They're monsters. They live in this forest but sometimes they come out and threaten my village. They don't really do anything but grow as they eat plants and things and then split when they get big enough," Alice explains.

Twinkaleni gives a skeptical, "Hmm."

"Well, what do you say they are?" Alice asks the Murin.

Danahlia answers before her, "She doesn't know."

Twinkaleni makes an irritated squeak saying, "I believe I told you that they were gelatinous semi-translucent semi-sentient beings of undefinable origin or purpose."

Danahlia hooks a thumb at her, "See?"

"Do you think they're magic? Could you feel one and check for a... ah aura?" Alice asks, eager to test her theory.

The mouse goes 'uh' and Danahlia chortles, "She's never gotten near one. She's too scared."

Twinkaleni places her pink hands on her hips, "Pardon me for being less than half your height, a forth your weight, and having only a portion of your reach."

Danahlia gets over her fit and extends placating hands to her tiny companion, "Calm down, Twinkie. With Alice here we'll finally be able to take one out. Then you can touch it all you want."

Twinkaleni narrows her eyes at the much larger girl and then remarks to the Tokala, "I am rather curious as to how you manage to vanquish these creatures. They've been a bother ever since we've arrived."

"Alright, I'll show you. I'm here to gather some cores anyway. Let's go find one," Alice suggests, and the trio sets off.

"How long have you been in the forest?" She asks as they search the underbrush for signs of jellies.

"Just a few days," Danahlia answers peeking over some bushes, "Hey, there's one."

Alice maneuvers around the bush to find a decent sized red jelly, "This is great! The red ones are rare, their cores are worth more."

"Will you be needing our assistance?" Twinkaleni asks as Alice approaches the jelly, taking a two handed grip on her sword.

"I'll be alright, just watch out for anymore."

Danahlia and Twinkaleni keep their distance as Alice dispatches the creature with a few well-placed swings. This jelly was in the open, making it an easy target. Once she's flung enough of the outer goo away, she reaches in and plucks out a nice red core. The fox wipes the orb and her fingers clean on her pants and turns to show the prize to her companions.

"Well done, most impressive," Twinkaleni congratulates.

Danahlia wipes some red ooze from her arm, "Gross, these things stink."

Alice has to agree, this one did smell a bit different than the usual swampy stench. "Yeah, they can smell pretty bad. I think it has something to do with what they eat," the young hunter suggests.

"I think you may be right. Take a look at this," Twinkaleni waves the other two over having followed the jelly's moist trail back a few feet.

"Is that a bone?" Danahlia asks, peering at a slender pink curved shape in the dirt.

"I believe so," the mouse mage points further back, "There are several more, probably some hapless rodent or bird the creature managed to engulf."

"Jellies are usually so slow. How would it catch anything?" Alice wonders aloud looking at the trail.

Twinkaleni offers, "It may have been wounded, sleeping, or even dead already. I've noticed the jellies are silent, persistent predators."

"Yeah," Danahlia agrees, "They've snuck up on us a few times when we tried to rest or sleep."

Alice considers this and then hands Twinkaleni the eyeball sized red core stone, "Do you feel any magic in this?"

"Oh, yes," the Murin exclaims as she takes it and looks over the perfect sphere from all sides, "It's frail but surprisingly intricate, like a spider's web."

"What does that mean?" Danahlia asks, getting a closer look at the faintly glowing core.

"Mmm, I'm not entirely sure. But if I had to guess, I'd say it means these creatures are not a natural magical phenomenon, but where most likely constructed."

"Constructed?" Alice repeats, raising a brow.

Danahlia looks back at the piles of red goo, "You mean they were made? For what?"

Twinkaleni continues to look at the core stone as she explains, "This is entirely speculation mind you, but generally, constructs of magical origin are meant to serve a purpose for whoever conceived them."

"A magical servant?" the lizard girl asks.

"Perhaps, though I've read constructs have many uses such as simple labor, the carrying of messages, and sometimes have even served as soldiers."

Twinkaleni goes on looking at the puddled remains of the red jelly, "But, considering these creatures' simplistic behavior and form, I honestly can't imagine what they would be good for. It's entirely possible that they may have even been some kind of experiment or mistake on their creator's part."

As Alice tries to place the new ideas in with her preexisting experiences with the jellies,

Twinkaleni holds the red core up to her, "You say we can exchange these in your village for food?"

"Yeah, there's a trade post. I've been trading in these cores for years. You can get all kinds o' things if you have enough."

"Wags!" Danahlia cheers.

The Murin smiles, "That is good news. I think I've had all the bugs I can take. If you don't mind, I'd like to find some others. I have a few theories I'd like to test."

Alice accepts the core, delighted by the idea, "Yeah, that sounds great."

"Excellent," Twinkaleni nods and the trio head off to find more jellies, Alice's tail wagging happily.

It has been years since Alice had company while tracking jellies. The last was when her father was still around and teaching her a few basics of sword play before he was called away. Ashleigh had always wanted to accompany her but her mother would never allow it, which left Alice alone much of the time. She grew used to keeping to herself but had always secretly wished for someone to come with her. Someone to share the weight of the haul, someone to watch her back, and especially someone simply to talk to, and now she had two.

As they search the dense forest, Alice asks many questions, eager to know more about her new friends. She discovers that shortly after learning of her talent, Twinkaleni's parents sent her off to some sort of school meant to teach the magically gifted to master their powers.

"They really didn't have much choice," the robed mouse continues, "Parents who discover their children are gifted in such ways are obligated by the state to alert and hand them over to the Order of Thermathrogi to be trained."

"They had to give you up? Why?" Alice asks, thinking how terrible it must be for parents to have to surrender their young.

"We are taught that magic is a dangerous and corrupting force, and further, that we are especially dangerous for our ability to wield it. The Order of Thermathrogi was largely created to imprison and study those with the power to bend the forces of nature, but over time it became more like an institution for learning the art, if still a highly regulated one."

"Wow," Alice remarks, having never imagined such a thing could exist. The Tokala's interest peaked, she asks, "How did you get from there to here?"

Twinkaleni looks upward as if considering how to respond, "Oh, well, that is a rather long story."

"She ran away," Danahlia provides.

"Now, Danny, it's not quite as simple as that," Twinkaleni complains.

"I know, but that's the gist of it," the taller girl counters, shoving aside a protruding bush then pointing, "There's one."

Alice steps up, unsheathing her sword, but stops as Twinkaleni announces, "I'd like to try something first, if you don't mind."

The two larger girls share a look and then watch curiously as the Murin walks with purpose toward the green jelly. The creature is currently trying to envelope part of a small, wide leafed plant, and from the look of the part already decaying inside of it, it had been at it for a while. Twinkaleni approaches the jelly, circling it, observing.

She then holds out both palms toward the indifferent monster and calls, "Asendiote!"

Alice and Danahlia take a few steps toward their smaller companion, not wanting to miss a chance to see her magic at work.

Twinkaleni lifts her hands slowly as if holding a ball between her fingers. To Alice's amazement, the jelly begins to change its shape from a hemisphere to more of a cone, the peak of which has the jelly encased core.

Twinkaleni calls out again, "Gravitus asendiote!" and one of her hands shifts to appear as if pushing down on something flat while the other starts to shake still looking to be gripping an invisible ball.

The jelly steadily becomes a more defined cone as the core looks like it's trying to pull free by flying straight up from the main body. Twinkaleni lets out a strained gasp but then holds her breath, her arms shaking as she tries to maintain the spell. Suddenly, with a wet pop, the core shoots up into the air and Twinkaleni's arms drop limply, her shoulder slumping.

Danahlia runs over to the jelly calling, "I got it," and manages to catch the freed core just as it nearly falls back into the creature. The jelly begins to deflate, collapsing in on itself until it forms a smelly, slowly widening puddle.

"That was amazing!" Alice exclaims, taking a few steps toward Twinkaleni, who sways a bit on her feet while taking rapid exhausted breaths.

Alice offers one of her water skins and the little mouse girl accepts it with a grateful nod, taking a few swallows before returning it. Danahlia rejoins the others with the core and Twinkaleni holds out her hand for it.

"I'd like to... test something with that... if you please," she huffs.

Danahlia hands over the core and Twinkaleni takes it over to the jelly's remains. She kneels at the edge and extends the core over it.

Alice warns, "Be careful, you don't want to get that on you or your clothes."

Twinkaleni then wraps her loose robe sleeve around her arm and holds the core out to the center of the puddle. To the girls' amazement the goo starts to pull toward it, the puddle getting smaller and thicker as Twinkaleni moves the core closer. She pulls it away and the puddle widens, spreading out again. She then brings it closer once more. The drawing effect the core has on the goo gets steadily weaker until there's none at all.

"Fascinating," the little mage says, her breathing approaching normal. Alice had never tried such an experiment. Getting the cores was hard enough, she never considered trying to give them back.

"What'd you do that for?" Danahlia asks, coming up behind the Murin.

Twinkaleni moves the core over the non-responsive goo puddle as she answers, "I wanted to see if this corrosive gelatinous substance had any magical properties without touching it."

Alice approaches the pair, "Does it?"

"It appears to hold only a minute charge after the core is extracted. A charge that quickly dissipates, indicating the gelatinous mass of the jelly is not inherently magical but only the core. I'd like to run some more tests if you two are up for it."

"Yeah, sure!" Alice answers enthusiastically.

Danahlia nods, "Nothin' else to do."

It's getting late in the afternoon as the trio walk along in search for more jellies.

"How much can we get for the red and green cores we already have?" Danahlia asks looking around the forest.

Alice considers, "Split three ways, mmm, maybe three or four decent meals worth."

Danahlia looks at Alice, a little surprised, "That's all? I thought the red ones were worth a lot."

"It would be worth more to one, but divided by three, everything is smaller," says Twinkaleni.

"Oh ticks, we're gonna have to get a lot of 'em then," Danahlia groans as she grabs some kind of blue beetle from a downed tree trunk and pops it into her mouth.

She crunches on it audibly and Alice wonders, "Are those, good?"

"No," Twinkaleni assures her.

Though Danahlia goes on to say, "Some are better than others. Oh, like that big caterpillar guy where we met, those are the best. I love how they just burst in your mouth."

Twinkaleni makes a disgusted noise but Alice purses her lips, thinking she might want to try one at some point.

The girls find another green jelly, this one wandering aimlessly over some grass. "Twinkaleni, do you think you could use your magic to push the core off to the side?" Alice asks.

The mouse mage's eyebrows rise, "Oh, I think I know what you plan. I'll give it a try." Twinkaleni steps up and extends both her palms forward as if pushing a small ball away from her, calling out, "Telefuss."

In Alice's extensive experience, anytime a jelly is disturbed, its core often floats directly to its center, forcing anyone who wishes to get at it to go through much of its corrosive gelatin. But as Alice circles around this jelly, its core seems to be fighting some invisible force while trying to reach its middle. Unable to overcome the little mage's magic, it ends up being pushed to the far edge. The core wobbles indecisively as Alice prepares to make a heavy vertical strike.

She manages to slice off the edge with the core, separating it from the main body and then flicks her blade to send that bit a few inches away so as not to let it rejoin the main mass. The piece with the core stone takes the usual upside down bowl shape of the jelly almost immediately, though far smaller. Working quickly Alice slices away more of the jelly until she can safety reach in and claim the reward.

"Well struck. That took considerably less energy for the both of us," Twinkaleni congratulates, making the young fox smile.

"Great! We have a strategy to get these things," Danahlia cheers.

Twinkaleni nods, "Indeed, now we just have to find them."

"We should check near water, they like moist areas best," Alice suggests, and the girls continue their hunt.

As they walk, Alice passes around some bread and water, which the girls thank her for.

Searching and eating, Twinkaleni affirms, "We *will* repay you for this, Alice." She then nudges her larger friend in the thigh with an elbow, "Right, Danny?"

"Vo yeah," Danahlia adds with her mouth full.

Alice grins, "Don't worry about it," happy just to have them around, but then she wonders, "How have you managed without any supplies?"

"We did have a few things with us," Twinkaleni starts.

Then Danahlia finishes, "But those jelly creatures got to 'em when we were sleeping just after we got here. First time we saw 'em was when they were already digesting our water and what little was left of our food, sacks and all."

"Yes. I'm afraid we were starting to get rather desperate before your timely arrival, Alice. Honestly, I don't know what we would have done without your aid."

"That's alright, I'm usually, out here alone, so I'm... really, glad I met you two," Alice says, her eyes dropping to the ground as the last words come out a bit shaky for some reason.

Danahlia's arms wrap around Alice's torso and the lizard girl hugs her close, letting her actions speak for her. Alice is taken aback by the abruptness of the contact but then gives into it, putting her arms around Danahlia, feeling the taller girl's bread filled cheek on her forehead and her hands on her back. Twinkaleni smiles and a feeling of joy blooms in the young fox's heart. It radiates outward to warm her entire being and tells her that this is the beginning of something grand.

Chapter 3

Leaving

The sun is casting the forest in ember and shadow when the searching trio comes across a large pond. Jellies are scattered across the shore and it's exactly what Alice was hoping to find.

Danahlia pans a finger across the far side, "Wow, look at 'em all."

"Whiskers, if we can collect all their cores, we should be able to procure supplies enough to last us for some time," Twinkaleni adds excitedly.

Before Alice can agree, Danahlia starts forward, "Yeah, let's go get 'em."

"Hold on, it's getting late. I think we should find a tree for the night," Alice advises holding a hand over Danahlia's tail as it slides through her fingers.

"But they're right there," Danahlia counters, pointing her stick at a few of the closest jellies, dragging themselves lazily along the shore grasses.

"Don't worry, they'll be there tomorrow. Jellies like moist spots," Alice reminds.

Danahlia raises an eyebrow, though she doesn't have any hair on it, to Twinkaleni, who nods, "I agree with Alice. It would be dangerous and inefficient to find a safe tree in the dark."

Danahlia lifts her arms in concession, "Alright, let's go find us a tree."

Alice always slept in trees at night while in the forest. Jellies couldn't climb and it kept her safe from anything else that couldn't. She heads to the shore, easily avoiding an aimlessly wandering jelly, to top off her water supply and drink.

Danahlia approaches and asks tentatively, "Hey, Alice, so, you think I could try out your sword? I'm startin' to feel kinda like I'm not doing as much as I could, you know?"

Alice's immediate thought is no. In the past, many people, young and old, have shown interest in her prized possession, and in her experience, if she let them hold it, they generally had a hard time giving it back. But Alice knew what Danahlia meant and decides to extend her trust to her new friend.

The Tokala lifts the weapon from over her shoulder and hands Danahlia the sword, still in its sheath, but warns, "Be careful. It's really sharp, and heavier than it looks."

Danahlia's arms drop a bit from the weight. "Whoa, you weren't kiddin'. Wags, thanks, I'll bring it right back," she says, putting the sheath on her back and wielding the weapon in both hands.

Alice watches, a little knot of worry in her gut, as Danahlia approaches a dark green jelly a few yards away.

Twinkaleni takes her attention, pointing out a massive oak tree, "I believe this one should be able to sustain our weight." Alice agrees, admiring the solid trunk and thick low hanging branches that spread wide, nearly parallel to the ground for several yards. "Oh my," Twinkaleni remarks, looking over at Danahlia who whacks away at the jelly, sending dark green smelly goo everywhere.

A few minutes later, the tallest of the girls comes back, a mess of clinging goop, but smiles showing her companions an unblemished core stone.

While cleaning herself and the weapon, Danahlia chortles, "That was pretty fun. You should give it a try, Twinkie."

"I think I'd prefer my magic thank you," the diminutive mouse mage replies and Alice smiles, handing Danahlia her rag blouse to help the goo covered girl wash up.

True to her word, Danahlia gives Alice back her cleaned sword, wet blouse, and the core stone. Alice spots a bit of green slime standing out on Danahlia's brown skin and wipes it off, earning a grin.

After a small meal of bread and water, the girls retire to the safety of the tree. Twinkaleni holds onto Danahlia's back as the larger girl's clawed hands and taloned feet make for an easy assent. Climbing up after, Alice sees behind Twinkaleni's robe that the Murin's pink hairless tail ends in a ragged nub only a few inches from her rump.

"What happened to your tail?" she asks as the other two girls choose the lowest and thickest branch, Alice climbing to the next one up.

"Oh, I lost that when I fled the Order," Twinkaleni explains as she crawls to a Y in the branch to settle down on. "You see, the Order of Thermathrogi is entrusted with keeping the wielders of magic in check. Which generally means keeping us locked away in their great stone fortresses," she yawns but continues, "I fear every day that the Order may use my tail to track me down but since they haven't yet, I can only conclude that the war is taxing their resources sufficiently that hunting rogue magi is not a priority."

"You're being hunted?" Alice asks, making a safety line of the rope she brought.

"Mmm, possibly. It's one of the main reasons we came out to the country," Twinkaleni replies sleepily.

As Alice settles in, she feels something on her dangling tail and peers over her branch to Danahlia. The lizard girl is lying on her belly, her toe talons dug into the tree's trunk while her long tapered tail passes through Alice's as it lazily waves back and forth.

She smiles up at her over her shoulder, "So you live in a village with your parents?"

"Not exactly. My parents are... gone, I live near the village," Alice replies somberly.

"Were they taken by the war?" Danahlia asks, her tail dropping to sag.

"Yeah."

Danahlia looks away, "Mine too."

"How?"

Danahlia sighs, "We were in the wrong place at the wrong time when it started. Yours?"

"My dad was killed in the fighting, my mom died later from grief," Alice explains, trying not to think back to it, and looks over to Twinkaleni, who seems to already be asleep. "What about Twinkaleni, are her parents still around?"

"She doesn't know. She never went back to her home town. Thinks if that Order found out her parents were harboring her or knew anything, they might get hurt."

"That Order, thermothogee, doesn't seem very nice," Alice comments.

"Thermathrogi," Twinkaleni corrects without opening her eyes, "And no, they are not."

"Why did you leave it?" Alice asks.

Twinkaleni yawns again, "A story for another time."

The sun has gone down and Alice can only just make out the others by moon light.

Danahlia extends her tail up to Alice and grins, "Today was fun."

Alice gives her tail a reassuring squeeze, "Yeah. Goodnight, Danny."

Danahlia lets her tail fall away to hang loosely over the side of her branch, "Mmm, night, Alice."

Alice looks to the small patch of crescent shaped light on the mouse girl's ear, "Goodnight, Twinkaleni."

"Goodnight, Alice," Twinkaleni replies.

"Night, Twinkie," Danahlia calls and the mouse mage lets out a heavy breath. Tired, the girls fall quickly asleep.

The next morning, Alice is jolted awake and nearly falls from her branch, only just managing to wrap her legs around it as Danahlia cries, "Ahh, ssssss ahhhh!"

Alice clambers back to her perch and hears Twinkaleni squeak in panic, "What? What's happening?"

The sun is just coming up and Alice peers down to see the lizard girl on her back, holding her tail near its end. A brown jelly wobbles directly below her on the ground.

"That tick was sucking on my tail! Sssss owww!" she cries out, in obvious pain.

Alice dumps water from a skin onto her rag blouse and tosses it down to Danahlia shouting, "Here, clean it off quick!"

Twinkaleni reacts, taking up the wet garment and gently whipping off Danahlia's throbbing appendage.

The poor lizard girl wiggles in discomfort, "Ow, Twinkie, that's tender!"

"I'm sorry Danny, but we must to get this substance off or it'll only be worse," Twinkaleni says, patiently cleaning her friend.

Danahlia grits her teeth and bares it as Alice unties herself to climb down.

The young hunter reaches the ground and unsheathes her swords to dispatch the offending jelly but Danahlia snarls, "No, that one's mine."

Twinkaleni makes one last sweep over the tip of Danahlia's tail with the damp cloth as the lizard girl swings down to the ground, landing right beside the Tokala. Alice offers the angry lizard her sword and steps back just in time to avoid a shower of brown goo.

After a minute, Danahlia reaches into what's left and plucks out the core, "That was for my tail."

Danahlia turns and shows Alice the small brown orb with a smirk, just before the damp rag blouse plops onto her head.

"Clean yourself off before it starts to burn, Danny," Twinkaleni call down to her.

Alice barks a laugh, accepting the core. She wipes it off and places it into her shoulder bag with the others. She then helps the little mouse girl down the tree, Twinkaleni's short arms unable to get much of a grip on the wide trunk, while Danahlia cleans up. The girls eat most of what's left of Alice's bread for breakfast and immediately begin clearing the pond's shore of jellies.

The larger girls trade off using Alice's sword and Twinkaleni offers her magic when she can. The three use their previous strategy of Twinkaleni pushing the core off to the side while one of the others slices it away. This saves them energy and time, so by noon, the girls manage to gather a nice pile of cores in various colors.

"This is more than I've ever had!" Alice announces proudly, giving her nearly full shoulder bag a shake and enjoying the hefty weight.

"Perhaps we should head back to your village and restock our food stores," Twinkaleni suggests, looking at the one piece of bread they have left.

"Yeah, alright. We should be able to get loads for all these," Alice says happily, her tail wagging behind her.

Danahlia asks, wiping down her arm, "Do you think it'll be enough to get us some packs and water skins?"

"It should be, but we'll have to see what's in stock when we get there," Alice replies, gathering up her things.

"Great! Let's move out!" Danahlia orders, pointing east.

As the girls make their way to the edge of the forest, they share what's left of the bread, though a mouth full each does little to restore their strength. Even with their strategy, the morning's battles have worn them all out making their pace slow but steady. They take turns holding the heavy bag of cores, though it hinders Twinkaleni so much that it's handled mostly by Danahlia and Alice. The girls avoid any more encounters, making the trip back to the forest's edge fairly uneventful, except for when Alice watches Danahlia snatch up a rather large beetle to bite off half of it. The lizard girl offers the other half to Alice, but it's still moving legs make her refusal an easy one.

Danahlia shrugs and pops the rest into her mouth, crunching on it with evident relish.

Twinkaleni asks, "Are there other Liguna in your village?"

Alice raises an eyebrow, unfamiliar with the term, "Liguna?"

"Like me. You know, smooth, beautiful, and cold blooded," Danahlia says, running a hand down her side, hip, and thigh.

"Oh. No, you're the first I've ever seen," Alice replies, grinning as the girls near the fields.

The Murin nods, "I thought as much. Danny, you'll have to stay here. Alice and I will secure our supplies."

"Right," Danahlia says, slowing.

Alice turns, "Why can't she come with us?"

The mouse and lizard girls look to her in surprise, Twinkaleni asking, "How much do you know about the Blood War?"

Alice looks to her new friends, "The Blood War? Is that the one being fought now?"

"Oh, well, yes. Come now, we should hurry. It would be best not to leave Danny out here for too long." In an unusual show of fervor, Twinkaleni takes Alice by the wrist and leads her in the direction of the village across the open fields.

Alice allows herself to be taken, a little confused. She then considers her water skins have been empty for some time and calls back to Danahlia, pointing, "If you need water, there's a stream that way."

"Alright, good luck guys!" Danahlia waves.

As they leave Danahlia among the trees, Alice asks, "Why can't we take Danny? And what's that have to do with the war?"

Twinkaleni continues pulling Alice along, "Oh, where to begin. You are aware that before the war the prime nations shared a time of peace and prosperity."

"Sure," Alice replies, not really understanding but not wanting to hinder Twinkaleni's lesson.

To Alice, the conflict that claimed her father was simply, the war. She knew very little of it besides the general dislike for the very concept. Her little village, so far removed from it, received very little news and the younger villagers were generally kept ignorant of even that.

"Once the war broke out, people were divided chiefly into two dominate sides, with people of cold blood, like Danny, on one side and those with warm blood like us on the other. Because of this schism, the current war is commonly referred to as the War of Bloods or the Blood War."

Alice stops, forcing Twinkaleni to as well, "But... that means, Danny is... our enemy?"

"No, Alice, it's not as simple as that. Come now, she, our friend, is counting on us."

Alice shakes her head slowly, immobilized as visions of her father being cut down by people resembling Danahlia bombard her mind and then what happened to her mother-

"Alice! Danahlia had nothing to do with starting the war. Her parents were killed because of it too, just as yours were. They had nothing to do with it either, no one we know had anything to do with it or the violence it brought."

"But my dad, he-"

"This war, like any other, has claimed many lives, and will continue to do so. All people like us can do is try to survive it. Danny, you, and me, we were all made orphans by powers beyond our control. We have nothing to gain regardless of who wins this conflict, so why should it matter? We need to stick together. Danahlia is in danger every moment she waits on the edge of the forest for us. Now come along, we need to hurry."

Twinkaleni gives Alice's arm a tug and she begins to follow again, trying to sort through this new information.

"Wha, what started it?" she asks.

Twinkaleni looks back over her shoulder still leading Alice by the hand, "Many things I imagine, peace, chief among them."

"How is... that doesn't make sense."

Twinkaleni looks back toward the oncoming village as she explains, "During the peace before the war, the prime nations prospered. Naturally their populations grew. More people meant more land was needed for housing, agriculture, and so forth. Those along the border territories would push for more land, skirmishes broke out, these were minor and common but they were where it undoubtedly began. Animosity grew, spreading rapidly, and soon it became dangerous to cross between the prime nations in some places. Those that over saw these lands argued among themselves while steadily amassing arms and support. And then it happened."

"The king died?" Alice breathes, remembering the panic and anger that swept through the village when they had heard the news years ago.

"Indeed. Rumors spread that it was by unnatural causes, after all King Ghadhanfar was still in his youth and healthy at the time. Fingers were pointed and with the increasing tension between the cold blooded and warm combining with the fear and panic of a leaderless nation, old hatreds between us and them were rekindled. Rumors of the king's assassination by the Cold Bloods became the rallying cries for angry mobs that ignited a wave of murder along the border territories. Over the next several months, any Cold Bloods found in Warm Blood territory were hunted down and slaughtered."

"Danahlia…" Alice murmurs, nearly stumbling, having trouble keeping pace with the eager mouse as she takes it all in.

"Yes, her clan, her family, was on the wrong side when it happened. Everyone she knew was murdered. She's been in hiding ever since," Twinkaleni reveals solemnly.

"But... why doesn't she go back, to her people?" Alice asks, suddenly feeling incredibly foolish and terribly sorry for even thinking Danahlia could be an enemy.

"She can't. The borders between the prime nations are battlegrounds now. And if she were caught by our people, she'd be killed without mercy."

"Wha, what do we do?" Alice wonders aloud, her heart filling with worry.

"Now, we get what supplies we can and head back to the forest. She should be safe as long as she stays hidden. I imagine not many people go into monster infested forests these days."

This much was true at least and relieves Alice some as she picks up her pace.

It's late in the afternoon when the girls arrive at the village. Alice leads Twinkaleni to the well first, where they parch their dried throats and fill Alice's water skins. Then they hurry to Ms. Graysen's trading post.

Ashleigh comes running out the door as they approach, "Hi, Alice!" she waves and then falls to her knees before Twinkaleni gushing, "Oh cheese! Who's this?! She's so cute!"

Before Twinkaleni can back away, Ashleigh grabs her up and pulls her into a delighted hug.

Alice can't help but smile a bit as Twinkaleni pushes and squirms, squeaking, "Excuse me! Put me down at once!"

Ashleigh reluctantly lets the little mouse girl go, "Oh, I'm so sorry, but you're just so adorable, I, I couldn't resist!"

"Ashleigh, this is Twinkaleni. We met in the forest. Twinkaleni, this is Ashleigh, her mom runs the trade store," Alice introduces, gesturing to each in turn.

"Oh, even your name is cute!" Ashleigh coos and reaches for Twinkaleni's large ears.

The mage slaps her hand away squeaking, "That will do!" and then readjusts her robe.

Ashleigh groans in disappointment and then seems to remember Alice, "That was a quick trip. You're usually gone for a few days when you take one of your expeditions. Oh wow! You got all those cores already?!" she exclaims standing to peek into Alice's shoulder bag.

"Yeah, Twinkaleni helped. Is the store still open? We need to make some trades," Alice asks, looking into the open door of the shop.

"Yeah, yeah, come on," Ashleigh waves the two girls in, smiling down at Twinkaleni before shouting, "Mom! Alice's back and she's brought loads o' cores!"

As Alice steps up to the main counter, she places her bag atop it. A few cores fall out and roll around and she has to stops them with her arms before carefully placing them back on the pile. She then looks around at the newly crowded shelves, tables, wall hooks, and anywhere items can be placed.

Ms. Graysen herself emerges from what Alice knows is a small store room in the back and greets,

"Oh, hello Alice, did you bring me more, oh, oh my…" she gasps as her eyes find Alice's new haul. She sets down the covered woven basket she's carrying and hurries over, "How did you get so many?"

Alice smiles and points down towards Twinkaleni, who isn't quite tall enough to be seen over the counter, "My new friend helped."

Ms. Graysen leans over the counter top and spots the mouse mage, who looks up smiling as pleasantly as she can, "Oh, hello little one."

"Good evening, madam," Twinkaleni starts, "We wish to barter for some of your goods and we are rather pressed for time. Your assistance will be greatly appreciated."

Ms. Graysen's eyes widen a bit, "Why, yes, yes of course."

Meanwhile, Ashleigh had been rummaging through the cores and pulls one out, "Look mom. They even have red ones."

Ms. Graysen's eyes widen a bit more at this, "Goodness, you girls *have* been busy. Well, what do you need? Paxon came by this morning so we have a decent stock."

Mr. Paxon was the traveling merchant Ms. Graysen dealt with most often. Too old for war, the Caprican made his living traveling from town to town selling and buying goods.

"Looks like you cleaned 'im out," Alice says looking at all the new stuff.

The mother opossum joins her saying, "We did alright. He really likes your cores. Whiskers, is he going to be pleased when he comes back. So what is it you're looking for?"

Twinkaleni tugs on Alice's hand, "Aside from food, we need to replace the items we lost to the jellies, plus clothes and packs to carry it all."

Alice nods and the girls begin searching and asking for the necessary items. Meanwhile, Ashleigh counts the cores, including their various colors, to give her mother an idea of how much Alice's haul is worth. Ms. Graysen starts stacking supplies on her counter for them and while they work, Alice notices the usual sounds of the village getting steadily louder.

By the time their business is done, the girls have, among other things, three backpacks, a traveling cloak, some assorted extra clothes, a few new water skins, and all the food they can carry. As they try to figure out how to fit all their backpack and water skins straps on while still being able to walk, the noise outside has reached an angry pitch.

"You girls be careful," Ms. Graysen says when she goes to peer out the front window and then mumbles, "Now what is going on out there?" A few seconds later she murmurs loud enough for them all to hear, "Oh no."

"Momma, what's going on?" Ashleigh calls from the floor where she supposedly helps Twinkaleni adjust her pack, but instead seems more interesting in fondling the small girl's large ears.

"Stay in here, girls," Ms. Graysen orders as she leaves the shop. The urgency in her tone and departure alerts them and they all gather at the window. Many of the village's residents have gathered in the street, and Danahlia is held struggling among them.

"Who's that?" Ashleigh asks.

Twinkaleni squeaks, "Ticks! Alice, we *must* do something!"

"Oh, no," Alice gasps, "She's a friend, Ashleigh, we have to help her!"

The trio race out the door to a chorus of angry and fearful shouting just as Ms. Graysen approaches the small group surrounding Danahlia.

"What is all this?" the Didel demands.

A worried squirrel woman tells her as the girls gather around, "Oh Linda, they found this Liguna girl near the stream. They say she's a spy."

"She is no spy!" Twinkaleni asserts.

"She's our friend, Ms. Graysen," Alice adds.

The opossum mother turns toward them, "I thought I told you to stay inside!" She then shakes her head, "I'll deal with this," and marches into the growing crowd, Ashleigh following on her heels. More shouting erupts as they hear Ms. Graysen try to bring some order to the scene.

"She's a spy!" someone cries.

Ms. Graysen counters, "She's just a child!"

"I've heard the Cold Bloods use child spies!" another voice shouts.

Then another jeers, "You'd believe it if you heard frogs had wings!"

"If word gets out that we're harboring a Cold Blood, we'll all be hung for treason!" a panicked voice cries fearfully to a general agreement.

"They'll burn the village!" Another adds.

"We must turn her in to a guard patrol!" shouts another.

This is countered by, "When was the last time you saw a patrol? We need to deal with this ourselves!"

"And what is it exactly you purpose we do?!" Ms. Graysen's voice rings again.

"I say we kill the Liguna and be done with it," roars who Alice believes is Ms. Duncan.

"I'm not being part of any murder!" the panicky voice screeches.

As the adults argue, Alice and Twinkaleni work their way around the crowd trying to find a way through to Danahlia.

Shifting elbows and pressed bodies keep them from making much progress until Ashleigh reappears, "Guys, my mom said you have to get your friend outta here. The village is goin' nuts! She can't keep 'em distracted forever!"

She then turns and bites a woman on the waist making them jump, screaming, and knocking into another, creating an opening. Alice charges in, shoving as hard as she can to push to the center of the crowd, while Twinkaleni, too small and encumbered to make any headway, falls back.

Two women, a Caprican and a Houdain, have Danahlia by her arms and keep her still while the shouting continues.

"Let her go!" Alice snarls as viciously as she can, baring her canine teeth.

The dog woman looks at her in surprise, "Go away, Alice, this has nothing to do with you."

"Let her go, NOW!" Alice screams.

This attracts the attention of Ms. Duncan who turns from her argument with Ms. Graysen, "You! My boy said he saw you coming out of the forest with the Cold Blood!"

"I don't believe any of us here are foolish enough to believe a word that slips from your cubs mouth!" Ms. Graysen counters, retaking the bear mother's attention.

"I notice you've always been the one to defend this, wild child." Ms. Duncan roars back, pointing an accusing claw at Alice, "Now she's brought a Cold Blood spy into our village and you still defend her! I say you're a traitor to us all!"

Alice takes the opportunity bought by Ms. Graysen to draw her sword, despite the encumbrance of her newly acquired supplies, and swings it awkwardly at the women holding Danahlia hostage. The goat woman screams in surprise and fear, letting go and falling to her butt as Danahlia rips free from the other. Together the girls shove through the shocked crowd and find Twinkaleni waving them down the street.

Ms. Duncan roars from behind, "We can't let them escape! Get them!"

The massive Urock leads a portion of the gathered women in a chase to the edge of the village until her enormous girth taxes her too greatly to continue. The trio flees the halfhearted mob into the fields and heads straight for the forest. Danahlia takes most of Twinkaleni's newly bought gear so the overburdened Murin can keep pace as they run across the grassy plan between the village and the forest. Alice looks back to see only a few still chasing with a widening gap between them and their pursuers. The girls slow to a jog but keep it up until they reach the trees and no one is following.

Twinkaleni collapses to the ground as they all try to catch their breath, lungs burning with every inhale.

"Wha...What...what happened?" Alice manages to gasp.

"I... was thirsty... so I... went to... that stream," Danahlia huffs.

Alice takes a drink from a water skin, coughs as some finds its way into her heaving lungs, and passes it around.

Danahlia takes a drink and tries to explain, " I didn't... think anyone... saw me. And then... wham... it just happened... so fast... next thing I knew... I was bein' dragged into town."

"You fool! You should have waited for us... to return." Twinkaleni squeaks angrily after rising enough to take a drink.

"I know, I know... I'm sorry. I was just... so thirsty."

The girls rest a while, keeping watch over the fields for anyone approaching. The sun is setting and Alice feels sure no one will be after them in the dark.

"I'm so sorry, Alice," Twinkaleni says, shaking her head, "I never wanted to get you so deeply involved in this."

"Yeah, sorry Alice," Danahlia adds.

"It's alright," Alice says, still looking out across the dimming field.

"No, it isn't," Twinkaleni goes on, "We disrupted your entire way of life. Because of us, you may not be able to return to your village."

Alice considers this and knows it's probably true. Now that she was seen aiding a Cold Blooded "spy" she might not be able to set foot in Toki for a good while. The thought didn't bother her as much as she felt it should have, but the possibility of never seeing Ashleigh or her mother again, to see if they were alright, and most of all to thank them, weighs heavily on the young fox's heart.

Danahlia hip bumps her lightly, "Hey, you saved my skin back there. Thanks."

Alice smiles and then gets yanked off her feet as the larger girl grabs her up in a tail assisted bear hug.

Alice gasps and Danahlia rubs her cheek all over Alice's surprised face until she laughs, "Ok, ok! You're welcome."

"I think it would be prudent to seek a tree for the night," Twinkaleni advises as Danahlia lets herself be pushed away.

Alice returns to her look out, "Right, you guys find one. I'll meet up with you later."

Danahlia peers between Alice's pointed fox ears, "Why? What're you waitin' for?"

"I wanna get my tent. Here," Alice takes off her pack, water skins, and even her sword, handing them to Danahlia. She wants to be light and quick, the time she's been waiting for was almost here.

"Maybe we should go with you," the Liguna suggests.

But Alice darts out of the tree line tossing back, "No, I'll be fine, we'll meet up in a little bit."

Alice flies across the field at her top speed. She'd been waiting for the moment when the sun would be low enough that she wouldn't be spotted with the dark forest at her back but there was still enough light to see by. She makes it to the top of her hill under the tree to her tent without hearing any alarms being raised in the nearby village.

Still, she moves cautiously, freezing when she hears a sound, and then Ashleigh calling softly from inside her tent, "Alice? Alice is that you?" The opossum girl pokes her head out and grins, "Alice! I was hoping you'd come back tonight."

"Ash, what're you doin' here?" the surprised fox asks in a hoarse whisper, embracing her friend as she emerges from the tent.

"I wanted to say goodbye. After today I didn't think you'd be able to come back for a while," Ashleigh says over Alice's shoulder.

Alice sighs, "Yeah, it looks that way. How's your mom?"

"She's fine. Nearly everyone lost interest when you got out into the fields."

Relief floods over the young hunter, "I'm so glad to hear it. Thank her for me, and thank you." The two hug again and then Alice begins taking down her tent.

"How are your friends?" the opossum girl asks, untying the bit of twine Alice sometimes used to dry her clothes on.

"They're fine thanks to you. They're waitin' for me in the forest."

Ashleigh tucks the rolled up twine into one of Alice's trouser pockets, "That's great. What are you gonna do now?"

"I'm not sure. We'll have to figure something out," Alice says, hoisting her folded up tent under her arm.

Ashleigh laughs a little, though with a hint of sadness, "I always knew you'd go off on some grand adventure one day."

"You can come too, if you want," Alice offers, but she can see Ashleigh's shadowed head shake.

"I can't, my mom needs me. So... you have to have enough adventure for both of us, ok? Promise."

Alice does and they share one last hug. Ashleigh gives Alice a tight squeeze and they whisper their goodbyes. Then Alice sprints away back to the forest's edge. She looks back once, seeing Ashleigh's silhouette standing beside her tree on the hill and is gland its dark. She never liked anyone seeing her cry. As she races for the safety of the trees, she makes a vow to return one day and repay the Didels for everything.

By the time Alice is once again in the forest, it's too dark to see much of anything at all. She feels her way around, slowly and cautiously, hoping she won't have to make camp alone in pitch blackness.

"Alice?" Twinkaleni whispers from somewhere nearby.

Alice opens her eyes as wide as she can but it's of no help, "Yeah, where are you?"

Then the mouse mage calls, "Estraleete."

Something that looks like a star appears above the fox girl. As it drifts down to her, she sees that it's a tiny bluish white light that effectively illuminates the immediate area.

Alice watches it in wonder and raises a hand to touch it but Danahlia calls down, "We're up here, come on."

Alice follows her voice and sees them both on the thick branch of an oak, similar to the first one they spent a night on but a bit higher off the ground.

Their eyes glow in the faint summoned light, Twinkaleni holding her hands out toward the tiny star while Danahlia uses her tail to point, "There's a branch that should hold you right here."

Alice asks, "Why didn't you go deeper into the forest?"

"We wanted to wait for you," Danahlia calls down and Alice smiles up at them.

She can just make out Danahlia grinning back before Twinkaleni calls in a straining voice, "Please, hurry. I can't maintain this spell for much longer."

Alice only has one free hand and searches for a way to climb until Danahlia extends her tail down to her, "Here."

Alice is just tall enough to place the tent on the Liguna's long appendage. Danahlia wraps around it and brings it up as Alice quickly climbs up to a branch off to their right. The tiny light goes out with an exhausted huff from Twinkaleni, just as Alice settles on the branch.

Something bumps her shoulder and she feels around to Danahlia's tail wrapped around something small, "It's some bread and water."

"Thanks," Alice says to the darkness to her left, accepting the items.

All the excitement of the day has left her ravenous and she quickly digs into her dinner.

As she does, Danahlia comments, "So it looks like you're comin' with us."

"Looks like," Alice agrees.

Then she hears the joy in Danahlia's voice, "Welcome to the team."

Chapter 4

A Feast of Ants

The following morning as the sun just begins to rise, the girls climb down from their tree to gather at the base for breakfast and sort through their new gear. They all have backpacks loaded with food, mostly hard bread, a few fish, and their temporary wealth even allowed them to splurge on some cheese. Each girl has a few water skins and a small assortment of additional clothing as well.

"Here, this is for you," says Alice, handing the traveling cloak they bought to Danahlia.

She puts it on with the hood up and gives a little spin, "How do I look?"

Alice chortles, "Your tail's showin'."

Danahlia wraps it as best she can about her waist and one leg while Twinkaleni puts in, "As conspicuous as anyone wearing a cloak. But as long you're only seen from a distance, I believe it will serve to obfuscate your Liguna features. Still we must be cautious. Your feet would give you away to anyone looking."

Danahlia taps her large curved talons on a surface root, "Right, so what's our next move?"

Alice puts her pack on over her sword, "I don't think anyone is gonna come lookin' for us in here."

Twinkaleni rubs one of her large ears in thought, "And if I recall from our maps, this forest is particularly large, with several settlements close to its borders just like your village."

Alice's eyes widen in excitement, "You have maps?" Alice had never ventured far from Toki and thus had no idea what the rest of the world looked like.

"Mmm, not anymore. Jellies got those too," Danahlia answers glumly.

Twinkaleni nods, "Indeed, and I think it would be wise to stay within the wood until gossip of what transpired yesterday can be replaced by some other event."

"That's a plan. We can explore the forest awhile, we have enough food," Danahlia says encouragingly.

Alice adds, "We can get more cores to trade for when we leave."

Twinkaleni claps her small hands, "Then I believe we have our course of action."

With that the girls gather their things and head deeper into the forest.

"Maybe we should try to find that pond again, that was a good spot for jelly huntin'," Danahlia suggests.

Twinkaleni nods, "Having a fresh water source will be an asset."

"Yeah, we'll just have to find it again. Which way was it?" wonders Alice aloud.

Danahlia points in a westerly direction, "I think it was over there."

But Twinkaleni interjects, "I believe it was to the northwest of our present location."

Alice doesn't bother suggesting it was southwest.

"Alice, which way do you think it was?" Twinkaleni asks.

The Tokala shrugs, "I'm not all that sure, but I think we should head west for now, just to put some distance between us and Toki."

Danahlia grins at her and Twinkaleni considers for a moment before saying, "That is a prudent course. We need to find a source of water if we plan to stay out here for long."

Alice adds, "Our food won't last forever either, let's look for things we can eat."

The girls head west, for the most part. Danahlia spots a green jelly and asks Alice for her sword, but Twinkaleni advises against it, "We should establish a camp first before expending energy on eliminating these creatures. Carrying core stones around will only add to our weight."

"Oh come on, its right there," Danahlia whines.

The mouse mage concedes, "Oh very well, but we must pace ourselves. Who knows how long it will take to find a decent site."

Danahlia grins and Alice hands her the sword. The lizard girl reduces the jelly into a puddle in moments, bringing back a nice little green core. She wipes down the sword and the core with her cloak and the trio continue on, Danahlia leading while happily humming to herself.

"So how did you guys meet?" Alice asks.

Twinkaleni looks up, considering, "Oh, we rather literally bumped into each other."

"I almost stepped on her," Danahlia adds.

"What? How?" Alice asks amused as they walk through the woods.

"She's tiny," Danahlia calls back.

"I believe it requires a bit more explanation. You see, Danny had already been on her own for some time and I had just fled the Order. I was running through a forest much like this one, thinking the thick foliage would keep me hidden until I could plan my next move," reveals Twinkaleni.

Danahlia laughs, "Then you popped out right in front o' me and screamed just before I squished you."

"Yes, yes, it was the first time I had ever seen a Liguna. The war was already under way and well, she is quite a bit larger than I," explains Twinkaleni self-consciously.

Alice smiles as Danahlia goes on, "So she throws fire at me and I give her a bop on the head with my spear," the lizard girl shakes her long, if not dangerously pointed, stick, "Plan was to rob 'er, but she was just so cute and helpless, with her big ol' ears, and that tiny little pink nose, and-"

"We get it!" Twinkaleni squeaks, slapping at Danahlia's tail as it pokes around her face for emphasis.

Alice laughs.

Danahlia faces forward again and continues, "Anywho, she says she's on the run same as me and we've been at it ever since."

"Wow. How long have you been together?" Alice asks, watching another green jelly wobble along as they pass by.

The two look to each other and Danahlia replies, "Few months now."

"Nearly three," Twinkaleni corrects.

Danahlia looks surprised, "Really? Time flies."

"Why did you run away from that Order?" Alice asks the trailing mouse mage.

Twinkaleni says simply, "The war mostly."

Alice looks back at the usually talkative Murin, "What about it?"

Twinkaleni tugs on her ear, "I suppose I should provide a bit of context."

"Here we go," Danahlia announces.

Twinkaleni continues, "You may come to realize that magic is a powerful force and can be used for destructive ends as easily as not. And, as all power, it has ways of corrupting those who think they can control it."

"But you have magic," Alice interjects.

"While it is true I can manipulate the ambient forces of nature from time to time, I try not to lay any claim on the magic itself."

The fox girl raises an eyebrow, "Ambient forces of nature?"

"Oh yes. You can feel and see many of these forces, like the movement in a breeze, the heat of a fire, or the light of the stars. These are all forms of energy and when someone, such as myself, alters this energy, it is commonly referred to as magic," explains Twinkaleni.

"How come only people like you can use magic?" Alice asks, waving her hand around to feel the air.

"So far as I am aware, no one really knows why exactly. People seem to simply be born with this particular ability. I've read that some believed it was something passed down by blood. I've also heard that it depends on things such as the phases of the moon or the position of the stars at times of conception, birth, or periods of growth, all just hearsay really."

"So, no one can learn to use magic unless they were born with it?" Alice asks, a little disappointed.

"I do not believe so. As far as I know, one must be born with it."

Alice continues waving her hands around, "So what does it feel like, to… manipulate nature forces?"

Twinkaleni chortles, "We're getting well off the original question aren't we?"

"I don't mind," Danahlia calls from in front.

Twinkaleni looks to Alice who watches her with both pointed fox ears angled in interest. The Murin smiles, happy to have an attentive audience, for once, "Well, it feels somewhat like breathing I suppose, as there is an intake, a holding for altering, and then a release. Except instead of air going into your mouth and filling your lungs, energy flows in from wherever you call it, fills your being, and then is released, most commonly through the arms and out the palms or fingers."

"What do you mean, 'wherever you call it'?" Alice inquires, pointing and flexing her fingers experimentally.

"Oh, for example, the light spell I used last night so you could see us in the dark. Do you remember?" Twinkaleni asks.

Alice's eyes widen a bit, "Yeah, that was beautiful. How did you do that?"

Twinkaleni smiles, "Yes, mmm, basically I collected the light of the stars, but the light reflecting off the leaves fairly far above us, so it was an effort you know."

"Yeah, yeah, we're all very impressed with your light show," Danahlia smirks back.

Twinkaleni narrows her eyes at the Liguna before continuing, "Indeed. Well, then I simply formed that light into a ball and sent it down to you."

"That's amazing, Twinkaleni. I wish I could do magic," Alice bubbles, thinking of the possibilities.

Twinkaleni grins and continues her story, "As I was saying, magic is a powerful force, but granted to few. Naturally, those without the gift want it, and if they couldn't possess it themselves, they would control those that did. I learned this, shortly after the war began, to be the true reason the Order of

Thermathrogi was created. You see, the Order made sure to collect those with the touch of magic early so they could indoctrinate fresh minds that knew little of the world."

"Indoter...?" Alice stumbles over the unfamiliar word.

"Brainwash," Danahlia provides.

"Brainwash?" the Tokala raises a brow, "What's that?"

"Let me answer that with an example," Twinkaleni responds, "Imagine if, at the moment you were born, you were placed in a box that had no door, nor window, nor light, nothing but pitch blackness, save for a voice that spoke to you from outside the box. In such an environment, all you would know would be what the voice told you. You would not know your mother's gentle touch or even the sight of your father's smile, only the voice."

"That sounds terrible," Alice comments.

"To those who have enjoyed freedom, certainly, but to the one in the box who knows nothing else, it would be home. If the voice said there were horrible creatures outside that would tear them to shreds and that the only sanctuary is inside that very box, then the occupant would have little desire to leave it."

"But that's just lying."

"Quite right, but to the one in the box, it would be the only truth. That is something like what happens to those given to the Order of Thermathrogi."

"They put you in a box?" Alice asks in equal measures of horror and disbelief that something like this could even exist.

"Yes, a very large box made of stone, with many rooms and many doors, but no exits, not for us anyway," Twinkaleni says, her gaze on the ground before her.

"Was there a voice in there too?" Alice asks, not even sure she wants to know but still curious enough to let the mage go on.

"Oh yes, quite a few. I had several masters and they all had many pupils."

"What did *they* do, your masters?"

"At first, they told us that we were beings of evil. That our talent for magic was the result of our being the spawn of demons, and further, that we were then, ourselves, abominations unfit to live in this world."

"That's terrible! But couldn't you just look at yourself and see that you weren't? That you were just a kid?"

Twinkaleni shakes her head solemnly, "Remember Alice, inside the box, all you know is what the voice tells you."

"I can't believe something like this could be. How can parents let that happen to their children?" Alice asks, looking to both girls.

Danahlia shrugs, but Twinkaleni replies, "I imagine my parents were either forced or not told what exactly would happen to me. Perhaps spun some yarn about how I would be raised with the utmost care, given the best possible future, and assured that great things would come of me, but at the cost of never seeing them again. Who would refuse their child such opportunity in so difficult a world?"

"They lied to them too?" Alice asks, feeling the burn of anger for this Order she knew so little about but already hated.

The mouse girl shrugs, "Possibly, it's been too long. I don't really recall now."

Alice remembers Danahlia mentioning that Twinkaleni never saw her parents again and asks, "Do you remember anything about your parents?"

Twinkaleni tilts her head and tugs on her ear, "I believe I remember my mother. She was gray too, I think, and had large ears like mine. I feel like I can picture her singing to me but I, can't hear her voice anymore."

Alice turns and drops to her knees, grabbing the little mage up in a hug as tears threaten to roll down her cheeks, "Oh, Twinkaleni, that's so sad."

"Alice, please!" the mouse mage squeaks as she squirms uncomfortably in the fox's arms.

"Better get used to it, Twinkie, tellin' stories like that," Danahlia says with a sniff, she then joins in the hug, wrapping her tail around both girls and squeezing tight.

"Ladies, enough!" Twinkaleni squeaks again but both Alice and Danahlia rub their cheeks all over her face and massive ears. "Ok, ok! I think that will be all for my history today!"

Alice pulls away, "I'm sorry, Twinkaleni, but it's just so sad. I mean, I at least remember what my parents looked and sounded like."

"Me too," Danahlia frowns.

"But to not have even that," the fox girl gets teary eyed again and leans in for another hug.

Twinkaleni extends both of her short arms and shouts, "Whoa! Ok, we need to get back on track here. Danny, have you spotted any fresh water sources yet?"

"Eh-h, no," Danahlia replies hesitantly.

"Are we still headed west?"

"Y-y, maybe?"

"Maybe? What do you mean, I thought you were leading us west?!" Twinkaleni exclaims angrily.

"Ye-, well, I was, but then I became enthralled by your story. Look all we need to do is spot the sun and figure out which way it's setting," Danahlia says with a placating gesture.

Twinkaleni sighs.

The orange light cast in patches over the undergrowth tells them the sun is indeed setting, but the thick canopy of the forest makes it difficult to determine in which direction. The girls continue their trek in search of a clearing to check their heading by. As daylight fades, they still haven't found any and Twinkaleni suggests they find a tree for the night. By the time they manage to find one that will suit them it's nearly dusk. Tired from their day long hike, the girls share a meal at the base before climbing up into the thick branches to sleep.

Once Alice drifts off, she dreams. She is in a small room surrounded in blackness, save for a sliver of light shining under an imposing wooden door. Though she sees nothing, she knows the darkness is full of dangers, the kind that reach out from the shadows only to flitter away when caught in the periphery or wait under the bed to snatch at a carelessly dangling paw. She crawls to the sliver of light and wishes desperately that the door will open. Under it she can see the silhouettes of feet just on the other side. Then a voice calls through, the same one that announced the war had begun and had instructed her father to prepare to leave. Only this time, it calls for Alice.

She recoils as the door receives a solid knock and shrivels into a ball, terrified that she may be thrown into a horrible battle and be killed by savage lizard people. The knocking grows louder, more impatient. She can't move. The darkness of the box grows, seeking to swallow her up. The light under the door fades to black and she can see nothing, only hear the knocking at the door get louder and louder until it's thundering in her ears and she screams just to hear something, anything else. And then she's awake, holding tightly to her branch, shivering.

Her sharp ears pick up a noise, not knocking, but more of a shuffling, as if something were being shifted around. It's quite early, the forest in muted tones, when she peers over the branch to the ground where she suspects the noise is coming from. Her vision is still blurry from sleep, but she can make out something moving about the pile where the girls had left their inedible supplies. She rubs her eyes and blinks, then squints trying to get a clear visual. As her eyes slowly focus she can see that it is a very large ant.

It's bigger than any she'd ever seen. It appears dark gray in the early morning and is maybe as long as her forearm. Alice watches it for a moment, its short crooked antennae waving about as it crawls over their gear, perhaps in search of food. Its features are proportionate to the smaller ants she'd seen, though this ant's mandibles look viciously large just the same. Danahlia is asleep in the branch nearest and Alice tries to reach for her, but her arms are too short. She stretches a leg toward where Danahlia's tail hangs over the side of her own branch and waves her foot a bit while she hangs on tight to the bark of hers. Just before she's about to slide off, she manages to touch Danahlia's tail.

The lizard girl grumbles as the long appendage wraps around her branch and out of Alice's reach. Sighing, Alice looks down at the still exploring ant. She then unsheathes her sword and slaps Danahlia's butt with the flat of it.

The Liguna jumps, shouting, "Hey!" and looks around to find Alice grinning at her.

"Ugh, it's too early, Alice," the larger girl grumbles and puts her head back down.

"No, Danny, look!" Alice whispers hoarsely not wanting to disturb the ant while pointing it out with her sword.

Danahlia peers over her branch and then looks closer, "Oh, is that an ant?"

"Yeah, it's huge," Alice nods.

The lizard girl pokes the mouse mage, still snoozing a little further along the same branch, "Hey, Twinkie, wake up."

Twinkaleni's foot kicks a little but she doesn't wake. Danahlia smirks at Alice and crawls along the branch to position herself over the much smaller girl. She then takes a deep breath and blows hard into one of the Murin's large ears.

Twinkaleni squeaks in panic and nearly rolls off the branch but Danahlia catches her and kisses her on the forehead, grinning widely.

"Danny!? What are you doing?!" the angry mouse cries, tucking her knees in to push the Liguna away with her feet.

Danahlia and Alice laugh as Twinkaleni tries to clear out her ear.

"Alice found us some breakfast," Danahlia says excitedly, peering down at the ant.

Alice raises her eyebrows, "Breakfast?"

Danahlia looks to her in surprise, "You haven't had giant ant before?"

Alice shakes her head and Twinkaleni grumbles, "Great, more bugs."

"Come on, Twinkie, you like ants," Danahlia says making her way to the base of her branch.

Twinkaleni stretches, "Nghhh, I suppose they are one of the more appetizing of the insects."

Danahlia reaches the ground quickly and makes her way to the giant bug as Alice watches from her branch. The lizard girl simply picks up the ant by the thorax, its legs wiggling wildly, and pulls on its head until it pops free, "Let's get a fire goin'. Nothin' like flame roasted ant."

Alice lets out an approving, "Huh," at Danahlia's efficiency and begins climbing down the tree as well. She examines the two pieces of the ant on the ground where Danahlia left them before going off to join her in search of firewood.

They gather a few fallen branches, twigs, and dry leaves until Danahlia hurries back to their tree, clearly very excited about getting started. Alice follows. By the time they return, Twinkaleni has climbed down and is inspecting the ant. The two girls dump their firewood into a pile and Alice starts to rummage in her pack for her fire starters.

Just as she finds the little bits of flint and steel, Danahlia calls out, "Ok, Twinkie, do it!"

Alice turns and sees Danahlia has stacked their wood pile a little neater as Twinkaleni makes her way over to it.

"Very well, stand back," the mouse mage orders as she lifts a single finger to the center of the pile.

Danahlia hooks a thumb to Twinkaleni, "Check this out."

"Feasta," Twinkaleni commands and what looks like tiny tongues of flame emerge from the Murin's finger in a fast moving straight line into the pile. It lasts for only a second but is enough to ignite the dry leaves and start the fire.

"Wow, that was incredible!" Alice exclaims, knowing how long and how much effort it could take to start a fire herself.

Twinkaleni makes a satisfied noise and plops down to her rump. Danahlia adjusts the twigs and leaves, soon getting the fire up to a good size. She then uses her somewhat pointy stick to skewer the ant and sets it over the fire.

As Danahlia spins the ant slowly on her spear, Alice asks Twinkaleni, "Are those magic words?"

The mouse mage lies on her back and yawns, looking to the fox girl, "Mmm, not in the sense that saying them alone makes anything happen."

Alice replaces her fire starters and crawls over to the small girl to sit beside her, "So what are they for?"

"Well, when I manipulate energies, the intent of what I want to happen is very important for achieving the desired results. Having the results pictured clearly in my mind is helpful in forming the intent. The words I use, I've used many times and so whenever I say them, I immediately picture what I want the energy I've gathered to do. In this way, saying my phrases helps me form and channel the energy easier."

"Oh," Alice says, not entirely understanding, "Is it hard?"

"Let's just say it takes practice," Twinkaleni smiles.

"Legs are done," Danahlia announces, after snapping off one of the finger thick ant limbs and crunching on it. She then snaps off the other five, handing Alice and Twinkaleni two each and keeping the last for herself.

Alice watches as Danahlia munches with apparent relish and even Twinkaleni begins nibbling on hers. The Tokala brings one of the fire warm appendages to her nose and sniffs. It's different but not in a bad way, so she tries a bite. The exoskeleton is crunchy while the inside is soft and tastes almost like a lemon zesty chicken. It's quite good and she lets out a delighted 'mmm' that makes Danahlia grin. Alice finishes her ant legs and eagerly awaits more as Danahlia continues rotating the thorax and abdomen over the fire.

"What'd you think? Not bad huh?" the lizard girl asks.

"These are great!" Alice exclaims, "Think we can catch more?"

Danahlia laughs, "Sure, this one was a scout, so there's bound to be more 'round here somewhere."

From an adventuring stand point, this excites Alice. If they can find food, that's one more thing they won't need to risk trading for.

"But we should avoid them if we see them in force. Giant ants can be dangerous in numbers," Twinkaleni warns while she nibbles.

"That's true, but at least these gray one's don't have stingers. Not like those red ones, remember, Twinkie?" Danahlia asks, inspecting the cooking ant.

"Red ones?" Alice raises an eyebrow.

Danahlia taps the steaming ant parts with a claw, "Yeah, they were vicious, had poison stingers as long as your hand. Still good eatin' though."

"Indeed," Twinkaleni agrees.

"Ok, these are done," Danahlia announces proudly, sliding the thorax and abdomen off her spear with an unburnt stick.

She then gives each part a sharp tap with the stick and they burst open in a plume of steam. The insides of the ant have become a thick, mostly yellowish goop. Danahlia breaks off a piece of the exoskeleton and scoops up some of the goo. Strands trail behind showing how viscous the ant's inners have become as she brings it in to blow on it. After several blows she pops it into her mouth. Twinkaleni crawls over and does the same, so Alice imitates them. The goo has the same delicious flavor as the legs.

The girls quickly finish off the surprisingly delectable bug, Danahlia lifting up the last of the thorax like a bowl and sipping the rest of the goo before crunching on what's left. Twinkaleni pats her belly as a full Alice examines the remaining ant head. She runs a hand over the hooked mandibles, discovering that they are fairly sharp near the jagged ends and would make for a terrible bite, though the areas nearest the head are quite smooth. She grabs a smooth spot and pulls on a mandible. It takes effort and pulling in different directions before it pops off. Alice examines the freed mandible, noting that it might make a decent knife or even a saw if it were a little longer. As it was, the sharp jagged edge is about as long as her pinkie.

Alice picks up a stick and tries to saw through it with some success. Danahlia lets out a pleased sigh as she sits back on her elbows and kicks out the fire with some help from her tail.

The Liguna girl then looks over at Alice sawing, "The soldiers have really big jaws. Might be somethin' to look into if we can catch one."

"That would be difficult," says Twinkaleni, "The soldiers guard the workers and rarely travel alone."

"I know. I'm just sayin' if we *could* get one, their jaws might even be worth money," Danahlia grins.

"Could we sell them as food?" Alice wonders aloud.

Twinkaleni nods, "That might be a path worth exploring, if we can get enough and keep Danny from eating them all."

Danahlia rubs her tummy, "You can sure try."

Alice decides to keep the mandible and takes a drink from one of her skins. When she does, she realizes how low their water supply has gotten over the last day and a half, "We'd better start looking for water, guys. We don't wanna run dry out here."

Danahlia 'mmm's her agreement and rises, ensuring that the fire is out with a few handfuls of dirt. The girls gather their supplies and begin anew their search for water. Alice leads this time, at Twinkaleni's insistence.

As they press on, the girls encounter a green jelly and Danahlia asks Alice for her sword. The Tokala gives it to her and the lizard girl races off to dispatch the monster, retrieving its core with a grin. They see another a few minutes later, this one brown.

Alice steps up to take it but Twinkaleni calls for her to wait. "I'd like to run an experiment on this one. Danny I'll need that other core stone."

Danahlia hands it to her and the little mage maneuvers behind the jelly, though off to the side to avoid its goo trail. She then extends the green core to the brown jelly. Just before they touch, a bit of the brown jelly pulls away from the main body and extends toward the core. Twinkaleni pulls away and the brown jelly reforms into a near perfect hemisphere.

"Fascinating," the mouse mage mumbles as Alice and Danahlia look on.

"What does that mean?" Alice asks, staring at the brown core floating about in its bubble of goo.

"I have noticed that these creatures react very little, if at all, to external stimuli." Twinkaleni explains, while bringing the core to the goo again with the same result.

"Yeah, they don't care at all if they get stabbed or sliced or anything," Danahlia adds, poking the jelly with her stick. The jelly endures it, continuing on its slow way with no change in its behavior.

Twinkaleni slaps at Danahlia's stick, stopping her, and then goes on, "But it does show a clear reaction to another core stone. What I'm interested in now is if the core was taking the slime away, or was the brown jelly offering it."

Twinkaleni then places the core near the brown jelly again, but this time, when it reaches out for it, she lets it go and the core is quickly taken into the brown jelly's body. The two cores immediately seek opposite ends of the jelly and seem to push as if trying to escape their gelatinous confines.

Danahlia steps closer, "What'd you do that for?"

Twinkaleni watches with interest, "Wait and see."

"I think they're splittin'," Alice suggests.

She had seen jellies split before, but only when one core becomes two, creating two smaller jellies. She's never tried something like this and looks on in wonder. The two cores pull away from each other and slowly, the brown jelly begins to split neatly down the middle. This continues until there are two brown jellies, roughly half the size of the original, one with the green core. They continue to slowly move in the opposite directions that the cores where originally pulling in and the jellies soon part.

"Very interesting," remarks Twinkaleni.

Danahlia crosses her arms, unimpressed, "Great, now there's two. Can we get 'em already?"

Twinkaleni steps away to ponder and gives the larger girl a negligent wave, "I suppose so."

Danahlia makes a little cheer and she and Alice take one each, collecting the cores.

"So, what did you find out?" Alice asks, wiping her sword clean.

Twinkaleni rubs her ear in thought, "Well, it may be possible that the jelly creatures have some form of intelligence."

"No way," Danahlia says in passing disbelief as she wipes away some goo with Alice's damp rag blouse.

"Indeed. Despite my inability to determine if the core was taking from the jelly to protect itself, or if the jelly was offering it to protect one of its own, I believe we can, at the very least, conclude that they had some sort of social interaction. Though no doubt a very simple one."

"What does that mean?" Alice asks, looking at her new brown core.

"So far, all it means is that these creatures are more complex than I originally thought."

Danahlia makes a disinterested noise with her tongue that gets Twinkaleni to narrow her eyes at her, and the girls continue on their way.

Late in the afternoon, Alice points, her tail wagging, "Look!"

She directs them to a small pool nestled at the roots of a large tree and the girls cheer. The water is clear so they drink their fill of what's left in their skins before refilling them. They then wash a bit of the day off their fur and skin. The cool water feels wonderfully revitalizing on Alice's face. Danahlia and Twinkaleni seem to be enjoying themselves as well. Alice watches in amusement as Twinkaleni carefully cleans her large ears. As she does, she notices movement a ways beyond her in the forest and peers over the mouse mage. A few yards into the trees, she spots another giant ant and a jelly fighting.

"Hey guys, check that out," she points, waving her other hand to her companions.

Danahlia gets to her feet, "Alright! Two in one day!"

Alice rises as well, taking her sword in both hands as Twinkaleni squeaks, "Hold on, this may be educational," while tugging on Alice's tail. So they watch for a moment.

Fighting may have been too strong a term. The ant mindlessly bites with its sharp mandibles, but they appear to pass harmlessly through the green jelly. The jelly, in turn, simply moves into the ant until it envelopes most of the insect's head. The core of the jelly stays on the opposite side, keeping a safe distance from the attacker.

Danahlia gives Alice's shoulder a little push, "Get it before that blob takes it all."

Alice looks back at Twinkaleni, who doesn't object, and then approaches the two combatants. With a single swing, she separates the ant at the join to its thorax and claims it while the jelly absorbs the rest of the ant's head.

"Wags!" Danahlia cheers.

Twinkaleni adds, "Yes, well done," as Alice proudly brings back their supper.

The girls quickly gather some dry fallen branches and Twinkaleni uses her magic to set them ablaze. They fill their bellies with delicious giant ant and as Alice lies back on the ground beside her friends, she thinks if this is how they're going to eat in the forest, she might never want to leave. By the time they're done, the sun is setting and they find a suitable tree nearby to bed in.

Then a question pops into Alice's head, "Can those ants climb trees?"

"Oh yeah," Danahlia replies, as she kneels to let Twinkaleni climb onto her back, "I've seen 'em do it, though they generally stick to the ground unless somethin' lures 'em up."

The thought of waking up to a giant ant chewing on her unsettles the young fox as she climbs up after the pair.

Twinkaleni and Danahlia settle onto a branch together as they usually do while Alice takes one to herself close by. She ties herself to it with her rope and lies down on her back. Her tail hangs over the side of the branch and she soon feels Danahlia's batting at it gently.

She turns to look at the Liguna, who smiles back at her, "So where'd you get your sword?"

"My dad gave it to me," she replies, moving her thickly furred tail along Danahlia's smooth one.

"Wags, did he teach you how to use it too?"

"Yeah, he started anyway, but then he was called off to the war," Alice says, remembering the day the messenger came to summon ever able bodied man and boy.

"Was he good?"

"My mom said he was a great swordsman, and that people all over the kingdom used to pay him for training before he settled down," Alice replies proudly, though she had always secretly thought her mother may have been embellishing the truth a bit to make her feel better about his chances of returning home safe.

"What happened to 'im?"

"Danny! I'm sure that is something Alice would rather not discuss," admonishes Twinkaleni.

"It's ok. The letter we got said he died bravely covering a retreat for his men at some place called the Nearthrough Falls. Said he saved a lot o' lives," Alice says, recalling how many times she'd read the letter with her mother. She roles over then, suddenly not in a very talkative mood.

Twinkaleni chides, "Well done. What a wonderful memory to go to sleep on."

"I was just askin'," Danahlia shoots back and then says, "Sorry, Alice."

The young fox sighs, "It's not your fault. You didn't have anything to do with this war."

The girls say their goodnights and drift off to sleep just as real dark closes on them.

Chapter 5

The Great Clawed One

Alice is awoken, to what seems to her, a very short time later because of an irritating light flowing in through her shut eyes. She opens heavy lids to find a ball of blueish white light floating right before her nose. She waves a hand at it, mumbling, "Twinkaleni, cut it out."

The light evades her attempt to bat it away and then floats a little higher before darting off into the forest. Alice groans looking over at her friends but can't make them out through the spots in her vision and the blackness of the night, though she can hear Danahlia's light snoring. Alice sighs and falls back to sleep.

The following morning, the girls eat a breakfast of fairly stale bread from their stores and drink plenty of the little pool's water. The pool isn't anywhere near big enough to sustain them and they must move on.

As they walk, Alice asks Twinkaleni, "Were you using that starlight spell of yours last night?"

The Murin looks surprised, "No, why?"

"I saw a light. It woke me up. Looked just like the one you made. You guys didn't see it?"

They hadn't.

"A dream perhaps," Twinkaleni offers.

"Maybe," Alice replies but feels certain it wasn't.

A few hours into their daily hike, the girls come across a stream several yards wide. They cheer their good fortune and Danahlia drops her baggage, immediately stripping off her worn leather clothes. Alice hesitates for a bit but then decides to join her as the Liguna splashes into the water. Danahlia and Alice splash each other for a time before noticing Twinkaleni still on dry land, gathering their gear into a neat pile from where they dropped it.

Danahlia waves her over, "Come on, Twinkie, you don't have anythin' we haven't seen before!"

Twinkaleni watches and seems to consider for a few seconds before she takes off her robe, revealing her slim gray furred body, and begins walking carefully into the stream. It's not very deep, but if she sits in the middle, Alice finds she can submerge herself in the clear running water. The cool stream is enchanting on her aching muscles and she closes her eyes to enjoy it.

She's jolted from relaxing when Twinkaleni squeaks. Alice looks to see Danahlia splashing her liberally with water, until the little mouse cries, "Pavata!" making a swishing motion with both her arms.

A wave suddenly reaches up several feet from the calm waters in between the two girls and crashes over Danahlia with enough force to send her tumbling downstream. Alice laughs as Twinkaleni rubs her hands together and joins her in the center to bathe.

Danahlia pops up from the water coughing and shouts, "You win this one, Twinkie!"

As Alice watches Danahlia recover from the spell, she spots the same light that came to her in the night among the trees. It's faint in the daylight but unmistakable.

"Look! There it is again," she points. But the moment she does, it darts away.

Twinkaleni follows her finger and scans the forest, "What?"

"The light, the light I saw last night. It was just there."

Danahlia notices her pointing and looks too but it's long gone.

The Liguna splashes up to them and looks back to where Alice was pointing, "What're we lookin' at?"

Alice explains that she saw the light again.

"What exactly did it look like?" Twinkaleni asks, still searching.

Alice gestures with a hand, "It looked just like your starlight spell but every time I try to get a good look at it, it flies off."

"Huh," Danahlia huffs.

"What could it be?" Alice wonders aloud.

Twinkaleni purses her lips, "Hmm, it is possible that it could be some sort of pixie."

"What's that?" Alice asks, looking at the Murin as Danahlia plops into the water beside her, making little waves as she begins washing.

"From my studies, pixies are a diminutive faye people, many of which tend to have wings and flutter about forests. Though I did very little study on the lesser faye, I do recall reading that those who follow the light of pixies often become lost and are never heard from again."

"So they're evil?" Danahlia asks, rubbing down her feet and toe talons.

Twinkaleni settles down to wash up too, "That I can't say, but if you put yourself in the place of these tiny beings and had some lumbering giant following you, you may try to lose them in a forest, too."

Alice had never heard of, much less seen, pixies and continues to look around for the little light as she cleans her fur. While looking around the general area, she does manage to spot several jellies at various points along the stream. She points them out to her companions and Danahlia says she even saw some fish.

"If we can catch 'em, we'll have water, food, *and* jellies right here," Danahlia announces enthusiastically.

Twinkaleni nods, "This does seem an ideal spot for a camp."

"Wags!" Alice agrees merrily and the girls enjoy a relaxing time in the slow moving stream.

After they bathe, they do what they can to wash their clothes. Then, Danahlia and Twinkaleni scout out a perimeter while Alice stays by the shore to set up her tent beside a large oak tree. As she slowly raises her tiny dwelling, Alice sights the little blue light again, hovering close by. She pretends not to notice in the hope that her friends might come back in time to spot it. Every now and again, as she hammers a stake with a rock or ties off a line, she sees the little light bobbing around in her periphery. After a few minutes of watching her, she notices it settle on a branch and the light goes out. Once her tent is set up, she busies herself by bringing a few stones from the stream and sets them in a circle for a fire pit.

As Alice places the stones, she calls out without looking, "I know you're watchin' me."

She gets the response she was expecting, silence.

"I'm not gonna hurt you," she says loudly, but keeps her eyes on her work.

After she's done, she sits and looks at the center of the pit while keeping the spot where she saw the light go out in the corner of her eye.

"I just wanna know what you want," she says again, to seemingly no one at all.

She waits for a time but is given no reaction. She waits a little longer wondering if the thing had already left and she had simply missed it. Her patience ended, she suddenly turns and stares directly at the spot.

She sees a tiny figure no taller than her open hand. She can't make out details because the moment it sees her looking, the figure becomes a bluish orb of light and darts away.

"Hey, wait!" Alice shouts, swiftly rising to follow the light into the forest.

The light is incredibly agile, zipping through branches and weaving through the trees. Alice chases after it, having difficulty following as looking up to track it's position has her stumbling over rocks, roots, and underbrush. She kicks a stone and hot pain blooms into her toe. It radiates into her leg but she keeps on, determined to know why she's being watched. But as much as she tries, eventually the light disappears into the forest, leaving her winded and with a terribly throbbing foot.

"Ticks!" Alice shouts in frustrations, scanning around for any sign of the light while ignoring her pain as best she can.

Finding nothing, she sits down in the dirt to examine her toe. It isn't bleeding but still hurts enough that walking back to camp just now is unappealing. Catching her breath, she feels around her injury, wincing upon finding a particularly tender area. She manages to wiggle it and in doing so feels confident that it at least isn't broken. She then lies back on the ground and looks up at the thick forest canopy, taking slow deep breaths.

It's then that Alice hears a strange noise, like high pitched cries of urgency. Immediately thinking of her friends, she rises, angling her ears to determine the direction. Once she has it, she runs as fast as she can toward the cries. After a few steps, however, Alice considers that the voice doesn't really sound like either of her companions and also recalls what Twinkaleni had said about becoming lost from following such lights. She already isn't entirely sure where she is but knows the stream can't be far, plus the voice is calling from only a little ways off. Curiosity taking hold, Alice continues to follow the high pitched cries cautiously.

As she creeps along, looking up and around, the cries become somewhat intelligible. Its sounds like a tiny voice crying, "Say! Say!"

Rounding a thick tree's trunk she spots a disturbingly large spider web, spanning between two other tall trees. The tiny figure from before is caught in a low corner and seems to be trying to keep very still while calling out. The spinner of the web is a large, brown, hairy spider whose body is nearly as big as Alice's head, though its long slender legs make it look considerably larger. The moment Alice reveals herself, the tiny pixie goes silent as the large spider finishes wrapping some other unfortunate thing that has managed to get tangled in its impressive trap.

Alice had never been fond of spiders and seeing one so large makes her extremely uncomfortable. Even to the point of considering leaving the pixie to its fate simply so she didn't have to look at the eight-legged horror anymore. She didn't have her sword, as she lent it to Danahlia, which only added to her apprehension. The spider finishes its grizzly work and begins making its way rapidly to the other side of the web toward the pixie. The diminutive figure screams for help and starts to struggle in panic, its light blinking rapidly.

Alice acts, picking up a rock and hurling it at the spider. Her aim is off, but she does manage to put a hole in the web directly in front of the monster, making it halt. It waits as if in anticipation of another attack. Alice searches but can't find anymore rocks and not wanting to get any closer, she begins hurling handfuls of dirt. After enduring several of her ranged assaults, the spider drops down on a thread to the ground and flees. The pixie is left in a cloud of dust, coughing but alive. Alice watches the spider scramble up another tree some distance away before approaching the tiny captive.

"Are you hurt?" she asks, stepping closer.

When she does, the pixie starts to blink and cry out again, "Shae! Shae!"

"Calm down, I'm not gonna to hurt you," Alice assures the panicking little creature as she tries to get a closer look.

The pixie is anthropomorphic with a very slender, pale skinned figure, but she can't get any better details as the pixie's flashing makes Alice's head start to hurt and her vision blurry. As she squints through the haze, another light, this one green, flies into her face, making the Tokala fall back onto her butt. It comes at her again and Alice scoots away, her arms raised in defense. After a few seconds, she tentatively lowers them and sees the green light tear free the blue pixie and together they vanish into the forest.

Alice watches them go, her head beginning to clear. She rises, dusts herself off, and limps back to where she is fairly sure the stream should be. She manages to find it soon enough and looks along the shore hearing Danahlia and Twinkaleni calling for her.

Spotting them, the hurt fox shouts, "Over here!"

Seeing her limp, they rush over.

"What happened to you?" Danahlia exclaims, taking one of Alice's arms over her shoulder to help her walk.

Alice leans a little onto the Liguna, "I kicked a rock."

Danahlia grins, "What'd you do that for?"

"I didn't mean to," Alice insists as Twinkaleni catches up to them.

"Alice, what's wrong?" the Murin huffs.

Danahlia answers for her, "Alice's foot met a rock. It didn't go well."

"Oh, well, come on, let's get you back," Twinkaleni says and leads them to Alice's tent.

Alice is laid in their little camp. Twinkaleni begins poking and prodding at her foot, asking if it hurt. It did and after several kicks to her fingers, the Murin concludes that it probably isn't broken and advises that Alice stay off it for a while. Danahlia gives her toe a little kiss that makes Alice smile.

"Well, I'ma try to catch us some dinner, otherwise it'll be stale bread again tonight,"

Danahlia announces, taking up her spear. She then thinks for a moment before using Alice's sword to give her stick a proper point.

While she does, Twinkaleni chides, "You really shouldn't wander off like that without at least telling us. What if your injury was more severe?"

Alice sighs, "Yeah, sorry. But the light came back and I chased it. It *was* a pixie, I think."

Danahlia stops her whittling, "Really? What'd it look like?"

"It looked like a small pale person, but it kept blinking and I couldn't see it very well."

Twinkaleni rises, "Well, that does sound like a pixie, but it's gone now. Best to get some rest."

Alice lies back against a tree, watching Danahlia splash around in the water while tossing her newly sharpened spear about. If the Liguna is trying to fish, she isn't having much success but seems to be enjoying herself. Twinkaleni gathers a few sticks and piles them into the fire pit. She then stands to watch Danahlia and shakes her head. The mouse mage wades out into the stream to say something to the larger girl. Alice is too far away to hear but after a moment's search, Twinkaleni uses her water wave spell to send two fish splashing ashore. Danahlia skewers them both before they can flop back into the stream and waves them excitedly to Alice. Alice gives her a wide smile and waves back.

After some effort, Alice has a fire going with her flint and steel. She then limps around preparing several piles of large green leaves as Danahlia and Twinkaleni bring back a few good sized fish.

"Great job, guys. We could probably use a few more. I'll start cleanin' 'em," says Alice, taking the catch.

Alice knew a little about fish, if not fishing, and uses the ant mandible she retrieved before to descale and even gut the girl's dinner. Twinkaleni and Danahlia watch as she places the cleaned and gutted fish on a pile of leaves, while putting the guts on another. They smile at each other, and then head out to catch some more.

By evening, they have a decent meal cooking over the fire and Alice asks Danahlia to scatter the leftover guts into the stream.

She looks at the pile of entrails in disgust, "Uh, why?"

"They might attract more fish for tomorrow," Alice explains.

The possibility of more food immediately warms her to the idea and Danahlia grabs up the pile as best she can in the leaves. She then hurries down to the stream and tosses them in with a *sploosh*. It wasn't exactly what Alice had in mind but it would do. Twinkaleni checks on Alice's toe, which is still tender but at least not throbbing as before.

"How does it feel?" the mouse mage asks, gently feeling about it with her warm, little, furless hands.

Alice wiggles the toe, "Better, thanks."

"That is a relief," says Twinkaleni, reaching into her robe to produce three green cores.

"Where'd you get those?" Alice wonders.

Twinkaleni positions them equally apart around the fire, "Danny insisted we take them when we scouted the area. She said we should start collecting for when we need to go out and trade."

Alice smiles and Danahlia comes back after thoroughly washing her hands, "Food ready yet?"

Alice takes in a deep breath through her nose, "Mmm, smells like it."

The trio had worked up quite a hunger over the course of the day and sit around the fire to eat their fill of fish. Though some are burnt and others aren't entirely cooked, they don't mind at all.

By the time they finish the meal, it's getting dark and the fire low. The girls put their gear inside Alice's tent for safe keeping and climb up their tree for the night. Alice's toe aches a little from the climb but she manages and they settle in.

"Tomorrow, we should try to explore the area more and locate other possible food sources," Twinkaleni suggests and the other two agree.

Then Danahlia points, her silhouette only just visible, "Look, there!"

They spot the blue light that Alice had seen along with a green one on the opposite side of the stream, their glows bright in the dark.

"That's them!" Alice exclaims.

Twinkaleni peers at them, "Oh, I wonder what they want?"

"They better not steal our stuff," Danahlia asserts.

The green light seems to run into the blue before they both disappear into the night.

"What else do you know about pixies?" Alice asks Twinkaleni, watching after the two while laying back on her branch.

"Not much I'm afraid, other than they are considered lesser faye," the mouse mage answers from somewhere in the dark.

Alice yawns, "What's faye?"

"Faye or fairies are creatures that supposedly come from Fayelindran, the spirit world." Twinkaleni explains.

Danahlia asks, "Spirit world?"

"Mm-hm. It is believed by some that the spirit world and our mortal world merge at certain points and times, allowing beings to cross over from either side," Twinkaleni yawns but continues, "They even say magic comes from the spirit world and those of us who can wield it are touched by fairies or even have faye blood in them."

Danahlia shifts in the darkness, "You have fairy blood inside you?"

Twinkaleni gives a tired little laugh, "Perhaps. It's as good (yawn) an explanation as any I've heard."

Alice tries to keep awake, very interested in this talk of magical beings from another world. She forces her eyes to stay open, focused on the three glowing cores surrounding the embers of their fire. However, the more she tries, the more they want to close. She lets them, certain she can keep listening, only to quickly fall asleep.

Alice wakes before dawn to Danahlia poking her in the shoulder with the tip of her long tail. The sleepy fox briefly considers grabbing and biting the bothersome appendage, but merely bats it away.

"Alice, look," the Liguna whispers hoarsely.

Alice rolls to her side and finds both Twinkaleni and Danahlia staring intently at something by the stream.

Danahlia asks, keeping her voice low, "What *is* that?"

Alice rubs her eyes and follows their gazes to what is the largest mud crab she had ever seen. Crabs were a rare delicacy in Toki, so she knew what it was, but this one was unbelievably huge, perhaps even as large as Twinkaleni.

The giant crab is staying in the general area where the girls had tossed the leftovers from their meal the night before. The outer shell of the monster is a speckled brown and it has two imposing claws held loosely halfway in the water while it scuttles around on eight legs, each as thick as Alice's arm. It has too large white globes for eyes sticking up on stalks and seems to be busy feeding with its back to the girls.

"It's a crab," Alice whispers and the others look over to her.

"A what?" Twinkaleni asks.

"A crab. They live near the water, but I've never seen one so big."

Danahlia whispers, "Is it dangerous?"

"Uh, well, you can eat 'em."

That seems to settle things for the Liguna, who starts to scramble down the tree, "Great, let's get it."

"Danny! Do you see those pincer-like appendages?" Twinkaleni squeaks in warning.

"Yeah, definitely want to avoid getting clipped by those," Alice adds, following the lizard girl down.

"Got it, don't let those near me," calls up Danahalia.

"Guys?!" Twinkaleni whines from her perch in the tree.

"Come on, Twinkie, we can take 'im," Danahlia assures as she reaches the ground, "Plus, I never had crab before."

Twinkaleni lets out a frustrated huff and starts down as well.

Alice takes a two handed grip on her sword as Danahlia angles her spear at the monstrous crustacean. They approach cautiously and quietly, a few feet from each other as to hit it from two sides. Danahlia gives her a nod and Alice charges forward to give the creature a massive overhand chop. Her feet splashing in the shallow water gives her away and the crab begins to turn, raising its formidable claws while making angry clicking noises.

Alice hesitates for a fraction of a second as the fierce looking creature turns to her, and her blow deflects off the side of a thickly armored claw. Alice is pushed back to the muddy ground, open pincers reaching for her.

Danahlia shouts, "Alice!" and begins haring the crab with thrusts to its mouth with her spear. The wooden point lacks the power to penetrate the crab's carapace but does distract it enough for Alice to find her feet again.

"I think we made it mad!" Danahlia calls out as she takes steps back, the crab grabbing the haft of her spear while reaching for her legs with its free claw. Alice dashes back into the battle and takes off one of the crabs rear legs with a diagonal slice that splashes into the stream. The crab is undeterred and chases after Danahlia, who lets go of her spear and starts to run away.

"Danny! Lead it over here!" Twinkaleni shouts and Alice sees her lifting a large stone with her magic. Danahlia switches directions, sprinting right for the little mage. The moment the Liguna passes her, Twinkaleni cries, "Telefuss!"

The stone flies forth with incredible speed, smashing into the crab's face with such force that the creature is knocked onto its back. The legs of the creature flail about as its vulnerable, near-white, belly is revealed. Alice takes the opening and leaps onto the crab, shoving her blade downward through the shell and into where she thinks its brain might be. Even so, the legs continue to kick and pincers grab. Alice half slips half jumps away, leaving her sword inside the monster.

Twinkaleni falls to her knees in exhaustion and Danahlia kneels by her side.

Alice watches the crab's flailing slow until it stops and then checks on her friends, "Is she alright?"

"Yeah, just a little winded. Get some water will ya?" Danahlia asks, holding a rapidly breathing Twinkaleni against her chest.

Alice quickly retrieves a few water skins from their supply and gives the girls one each while keeping the last for herself. They all drink and slowly let the adrenaline work its way out of their bodies. The spell the mouse girl used seems to have taxed her greatly and the girls decide to sit a while.

Danahlia looks over at the crab, "Is it dead?"

"I think so. Let's give it another minute," Alice advises and takes another drink.

Once Twinkaleni is back on her feet, they approach the still crustacean. Danahlia retrieves her spear and pokes at it to no effect.

Alice steps closer and Twinkaleni warns, "Mind the claws."

Alice nods and quickly taps the handle of her sword before retreating, but the crab doesn't even twitch. They let out a collective breath and Alice pulls free her sword, strange blueish blood leaking from the wound.

"So, how do we eat this guy?" Danahlia asks, poking at the dead crab with her spear some more.

"We should cook it. Let's get it closer to the fire pit," Alice answers.

Danahlia and Alice take a claw each and drag the heavy creature back to their camp while Twinkaleni retrieves the leg Alice hacked off before it drifts further downstream. Once they have it there, the two larger girls gather firewood and Twinkaleni uses her magic to set it ablaze.

They cook the dismembered leg first, setting it directly on the fire until it changes from brown to orange. Using a rock from the river, Alice smashes open a segment and pulls out the steaming white meat. She hands it around and the others grab some too. Twinkaleni and Danahlia sniff and watch Alice eat hers before trying some themselves. The crab is excellent, fresh, sweet, and soft.

"Wow, this is good," Danahlia comments, and Twinkaleni nods enthusiastically, stuffing her mouth.

"Eat up, we got plenty," Alice grins, and before they've finished off the first leg, she hacks off another to set over the fire.

Twinkaleni looks over to the rest of the crab, "Alice, how long do you think this will keep?"

"Mmm, not long. I think we need to eat as much as we can before it goes bad."

"Great!" Danahlia says happily, breaking open another segment.

The girls eat their fill and only get through four of the legs, leaving the other four, the claws, and the main body still intact. As they all lay back, patting their stomachs in satisfaction, they agree that today will be a nice relaxing one.

"Oh look. That pixie thing's back," Danahlia says, pointing.

Alice rises to her elbows and sees the blue light hovering over the water near their side of the stream. The girls watch it for a moment and this time it doesn't flee. The green one appears from somewhere over it and swoops down, circling the blue.

"Hello?" Alice tries and the two pixies stop, then the green gets behind the blue and they slowly approach.

The girls don't move, afraid any shift might startle the tiny creatures into flying off again. The green one stops, still a few yards away. The blue continues until it's just feet from Alice.

The girls jump when the green pixie shouts, revealing it to be female, "Go on, Tally!"

The blue one bobs in the air as if fighting the urge to flee but then blurts, "Thank you. Save me from the weaver you did."

They pronounce their words in an unusual way, emphasizing different syllables. The girls learn little else as the little light immediately rejoins the other and they start to fly away.

Alice calls out, "Wait! Please, don't go." But they disappear into the forest.

"That was interesting," Twinkaleni remarks, as both girls look to Alice.

"What was that about?" Danahlia wonders.

"Uh, I guess I saved that one from a spider yesterday. That was when I hurt my foot," Alice explains.

"Very interesting," Twinkaleni says again.

Alice decides to cook the rest of the crab, thinking it will last longer and be ready to eat whenever they get hungry.

Danahlia puts a cylindrical bit of the crab's shell over her forearm and taps it, "I wonder if we can use this for something."

"Yes, I believe this might make a better spear point for you, Danny," says Twinkaleni, handing her the pointed end of one of the crab's legs.

Danahlia takes the pointy bit of carapace and sticks the end of her spear into it, "Hey yeah, now I just need a way to stick it on here. I need a pine tree."

"What for?" asks Alice, turning another of the crabs legs over the fire.

"To get some sap. I know how to make glue from pine sap and charcoal. Can I borrow your sword again?"

Alice gives her weapon to the Liguna and she runs off to a nearby pine tree. Alice and Twinkaleni watch as she cuts a few low branches and then goes to another to do the same.

Twinkaleni takes a stick from the firewood pile and inserts it into one of the hollowed bits of crab leg, saying to herself, "I wonder," and then to Alice she asks, "Do you think this would penetrate a jelly?" offering the jagged broken end of crab leg.

Alice tests it with a finger, finding the edges to be sharp and sturdy, "I think so. What're you plannin' to do with it?"

"Mmm, let's see how Danny's endeavor fares first, but I do believe we can craft some useful items with this creature's remains," the mouse mage says, toying with the two pieces some more.

By evening, Alice has cooked the crab's limbs and places the main body over the fire. Twinkaleni has crushed some of the charred wood into powder at Danahlia's request and the Liguna herself has managed to collect a cup or more of the pine tree's syrupy sap. Danahlia now mixes the sap with the powdered charcoal as Alice and Twinkaleni watch. Doing so makes a black and extremely viscous paste. Danahlia applies it generously to the end of her spear and then shoves on the pointed crab leg end.

As the Liguna rotates the piece over the fire, Alice asks, "How'd you learn to do that?"

"My dad taught me," she grins proudly as the glue mixture softens in the heat. Danahlia then stands her new viciously pointed spear up beside a tree, "Once that cools it should be pretty solid."

"Wags," Alice smiles, "What else can we make?"

"If that sap holds, I have an idea for something that might make extracting cores from jellies easier," Twinkaleni answers, "But I require a long stick like your spear."

"We should be able to find you one," Danahlia nods.

"And I think once we clean out this bit, the shell will make a nice big bowl," Alice adds, prodding the cooking crab's body.

"A bowl would be useful," says Twinkaleni.

The girls settle down around the fire, eating their fill of delicious crab while discussing all the things they could make with what was available around them, some practical, some not so much.

As evening turns to night, the girls climb up into their tree.

"Armor might be a bit beyond us, Danny," admits Twinkaleni.

Danahlia argues, "We could totally make armor. We just need to bend and shape the crab's limbs some to fit over our arms and legs."

As Alice ties herself to her branch she adds, "The edges are pretty sharp, we'd have to wear something under them to keep those from cutting into us."

"Yeah, yeah," Danahlia nods enthusiastically.

"And what would we use for this buffer? We certainly don't have the clothes to spare on such an effort," Twinkaleni points out as she crawls to a spot on her branch to sleep on.

"We could, uhh, hmm..." Danahlia trails off rolling to her back, her tail waving lazily over the side of her branch.

"I believe our most immediate concern should be shelter. What if it rains?" presses the Murin.

Alice agrees, "That's true, my little tent can't hold us all."

"Alright, alright, forget armor for now. We need to build a house," concedes Danahlia.

"Do we know how to do that?" asks Twinkaleni.

"I'm sure we can figure somethin' out," Danahlia answers confidently.

"Yeah, how hard could it be," Alice adds, picturing a little log cabin in the middle of the woods, complete with a door and even a little window.

Chapter 6

The Jellybane

After failing miserably once more at trying to make a frame work for a wall, Alice concludes, "We need rope, and maybe some more o' that sap glue."

Twinkaleni examines the rope Alice had been using as a safety line. It's much too short for building a house but the little mage hits on something.

She strips a stick of its bark in one long yank and begins pulling the soft wood apart into thin, curling threads, "I've noticed the younger branches of this particular tree are quite fibrous. If we can extract lengths of these fibers, perhaps we can weave them into additional rope."

"That's great, Twinkaleni. I'll go cut some more," Alice smiles, rising with her sword.

Danahlia gets up too, "I can make some more glue."

The Murin mage nods, "Excellent. I'll see about weaving these fibers together, and maybe we'll be able to get a simple shelter built."

Feeling like progress is finally being made, Alice wanders out into the forest in search of the right trees. Managing to find one, she cuts a few of the longer branches where she can reach. Letting them drag behind her in one hand, she goes off in search for more. As she does, some instinct tells her to turn around. Spinning abruptly, she startles the little blue pixie that was following a few feet away. It zips well over head for a moment before tentatively flying back down.

"Oh, it's you again," Alice looks at it, a little surprised, "Aren't you gonna fly off?"

The pixie hovers silently, its light pulsing.

Alice is about to return to her work when the little pixie asks, "What are you doing?"

Alice turns back to it, the light still hovering well out of reach, "I'm collectin' some wood."

It hovers just a little lower, "Why?"

"So my friends and I can build some shelter," Alice replies, looking at the creature curiously.

"Mean to stay in the forest do you?"

"Yeah, maybe, is that a problem?" Alice asks, beginning to feel a strange fuzziness in her thoughts.

The pixie flies in circles, "Oh no, Alice Jellybane, is most welcome."

The fuzziness turns to dizziness, "Wha, what did you call me?"

"Alice?"

"No, the other... hey, can you turn off your light?"

The pixie hovers for a moment more before her light begins to dim, fading until it's gone.

Alice's thoughts begin to clear, "That's better, thanks. Now what did you call me before? Not Alice, the other part."

"Jellybane?"

"Yeah. What is that?"

The tiny figure seems perplexed, "You it is. For some time, vanquished the dreaded jellies you have. Once, many of your kind fought them but now only you."

"You've been watching me?"

"Not I alone. Seen by many you have been. Spread your name has, to every twig and leaf. Known to us you are," the pixie says, fluttering in a circle.

Alice didn't know what to make of this. Apparently these pixies have been spying on her for quite a while.

Alice considers and then asks, "Your name's Tally? The green one called you that yesterday."

The pixie bobs in the air, "Taliantaquee."

Alice tries, "Tally-ant-que?

The pixie flutters closer on wings similar to a dragonfly's, "Taliantaquee, but call me Tally you may."

"Ok, Tally. Why have you been watching me?" wonders Alice.

Tally bobs up and down happily, "To see the Jellybane slay such monsters as the jellies, the biters, and even the great clawed one was most exciting. Less so when the weaver had me, but flee before you it did!"

"Huh, those creatures give you trouble too?" Alice asks, taking a new hold on her bundle of sticks and searching for another good tree.

"Oh yes. We are not great warriors as you are. Fight we do but small we are and can do little against the jellies especially," says Tally, following along.

Alice smirks at being called a great warrior, "So how do you survive out here?"

"We make our homes high and flee much of the time," the little winged figure admits.

Finding another tree with the right fibrous wood, Alice begins cutting off branches, "Ticks, that sounds difficult."

"Always has it been in the forest. But now, the only slayer of jellies you are and grown their numbers have."

Gathering her haul, Alice says, "Well, you're in luck, because my friends and I might have to stay in the forest a while and we plan to collect plenty o' core stones."

Tally's light flashes back on and Alice turns to watch her flutter in spirals, "Great news this is, tell my sister I must!"

"Your sister, is that the green one?"

"Yes, Shaelyantaquee she is," with that the little pixie abruptly flies off.

"Oh, hey!" Alice calls, eager to know more, but Tally is already gone. Hoping to see her again soon, Alice returns to her work and quickly gathers an arm load of stick for Twinkaleni.

When she returns to camp, she finds Danahlia mixing more of her glue while Twinkaleni has managed to weave a short bit of rope, or string at least. The mouse mage holds it up proudly as Alice approaches.

"Wow, that looks great. You think we can make more from these branches?" asks Alice, laying down her bundle.

Twinkaleni leans to inspect the new materials, "They should do well, thank you."

"So I ran into the pixie again," Alice tells her companions as she sits to examine Twinkaleni's string, "Sounds like they need help against the jellies."

Danahlia looks up from her stirring, "Yeah?"

Alice nods, "They been watchin' us and seem pretty glad we're fightin' monsters out here."

Twinkaleni takes one of the cut branches and begins stripping it into fibers, "Well done. We may be able to work out a mutually beneficial arrangement with these pixies."

Alice begins to imitate her, "What do you mean?"

"I'm sure the pixies know this forest well. If we help them by vanquishing monsters, perhaps we can get their help in return."

Danahlia's brow rises, "Hey yeah. They can tell us where to find food and water, maybe even like, a cave or something."

Twinkaleni perks up, "Oh yes, a water proof cave would be a significant improvement over any shelter we might construct with our limited experience."

Alice nods, "Alright, let's ask the next time we see 'em."

In agreement, the girls get to work on their tasks. Twinkaleni and Alice try to make rope while Danahlia prepares more sap glue. As they do, they go over questions they would like to ask the pixies.

So deep are they in their discussion that it's a surprise when Tally shouts, "Lots!" to Danahlia, who wonders how many of them there are in the forest.

They all jump, even the pixies, for Shaelyantaquee has come as well.

Alice looks up at the two faye, their lights out, "Tally, you're back."

The pale skinned pixie bobs up and down in the air, "Return I have, and with my sister."

The girls look to the other. Now without their lights and up close, they can see them clearly for the first time. They are both slender of body and limb with wings vaguely similar to dragonfly's, though pointed near the ends and especially thick where they protrude from their backs. They have no fur but hair sprouting from their heads. Tally sports a rather lengthy sky blue ponytail while her sister, Shae, has a short spikey cut of grass green. They both have large eyes similar, though darker in color, to their hair and extremely pale, almost luminous, skin. They wear clothes made from leaves to conceal their modesty and Shae has what might be a needle like sword but little else.

"It is nice to finally meet you. I am Twinkaleni Orbear," Twinkaleni bows a bit even though she's still seated. She then gestures to Danahlia, "And this is-"

"Danahlia Smoothide," Danahlia interrupts as she smiles and lifts a hand to flitter her fingers at the pixies, "But you can call me Danny."

"Shaelyantaquee I am, but Shae you may call me. And if friends of the Jellybane you are, then you too are most welcome in this forest," the green pixie bows graciously in the air.

"Beg your pardon?"

"Jellybane?" Twinkaleni and Danahlia blurt together.

"That's what they call me, Jellybane," Alice announces proudly, pointing a thumb at herself.

Danahlia chortles and even Twinkaleni visibly holds back a grin, "Interesting. How long have you been watching us?"

"New you are, but the Jellybane we have watched for some winters," replies Tally.

"Heh, the 'Jellybane' says you could use some help with the monsters in the forest," says Danahlia.

Shae gives her sister an admonishing look, "Yes. Some we can fend off, but persistent the jellies are, and more numerous they have become."

"Place trust in the Jellybane we can, sister. She has come to cleanse the forest," insists Tally.

"Uh, I can take a few, but I don't know about-" Alice starts but Twinkaleni quickly interjects.

"We can certainly help, if you are willing to aid us in return."

The pixie sisters look to each other and then to Twinkaleni.

"What aid could we offer such great warriors and one so gifted in magic?" Shae asks curiously.

"Like you said, we're new to the forest," Danahlia admits, "and we don't really know our way around yet. So if you could tell us where we can find food, that would help."

"And shelter," Twinkaleni nods.

"And other sources o' water," Alice adds.

The pixies look to each of them in turn and Tally bobs, "Oh yes, know the forest well we do. Help we-"

Shae pulls her sister by the arm, "Help we can but ask we must that you cleanse the spring of this river first."

The girls look to each other and then Twinkaleni inquires, "Cleanse it of what, exactly?"

This prompts the green haired pixie to say rather seriously, "Jellies."

The girls look to each other again, nodding all around, and then Alice announces, "Yeah, we can do that."

"Jellies are our specialty," Danahlia boasts with a grin.

Tally cheers and Shae nods her approval.

"Will it take us long to get there?" Twinkaleni wonders as they rise to gather their things.

"Not far is the spring," Tally assures them.

"I guess we can pack light then," Alice says, glancing at all their gear.

Danahlia nods and Alice watches as she takes her spear but also another long stick, this one with a jagged piece of crab leg on one end.

"What's that?" she asks, pointing to it.

"Twinkie made it, thinks it might help us get cores," Danahlia replies handing it to the Tokala.

Alice inspects the part with the crab leg. The stick is glued to the inside with some of Danahlia's pine sap charcoal mixture, though the crab leg extends beyond the end of the stick.

"This should be an adequate field test," says Twinkaleni.

As they set out to walk along the stream's edge, following the pixies, Alice asks, "So how does it work?"

"Well, my theory is, that if we were to thrust this end," Twinkaleni gestures to the crab shelled one, "into a jelly and scoop up its core, given that the core is large enough, it should become lodged inside. Then we can push it straight through the creature. Once the core is free, the jelly should collapse as we have seen before."

The two pixies have taken interest and hover around to listen.

Alice looks to the device approvingly, "Wags."

"If it works, we may have a new weapon to use against the jellies," the Murin concludes.

They come across a brown jelly wobbling along the shore line of the stream.

Danahlia extends her clawed hand to Alice, "Hey, lemme see the thingy. See if it works."

The fox trades her for the spear and Danahlia approaches the jelly. As she pushes the jagged edge into the monster's outer layer, the core lazily floats toward the middle of the mass. Danahlia has to angle herself but slowly approaches the core and manages to scoop it into the open end.

"Alright, now just push it all the way through," Twinkaleni instructs and Danahlia shoves until the jagged edge pokes free from the other side. They all watch intently as the Liguna thrusts most of the stick into the jelly, which moves toward the end a little before it starts to collapse. Danahlia stays put as the jelly loses its structure, spreading into a smelly puddle. A bit of goo drops out of the stick's crab leg end with the core.

Twinkaleni raises her little arms and cheers, "It worked!" then reigns herself in, "Yes, well, excellent."

"Ha! That was easy," Danahlia barks, stepping around the puddle to collect the core. "This is great. We'll be able to beat loads o' jellies now!"

Tally cheers enthusiastically as Shae looks on in disbelief, "To have defeated a jelly with such ease. Truly powerful you are."

While Danahlia cleans off the rather effective new weapon in the stream, she asks, "So, is the spring really important?"

"Very important it is, to us and our friends," exclaims Tally, bobbing up and down.

Shaelyantaquee adds, "Amassed there the jellies have."

As the party continues, the concentration of jellies increases and the girls cross over the shallow stream many times to clear the shores. They all take turns with the new weapon and even Twinkaleni is able to dispatch jellies with relative ease using it.

"Something this good needs a name," claims Alice.

"I was thinking, the core extraction probe," says Twinkaleni.

"Cep, for short," Danahlia puts in with a grin.

"Cep," Alice repeats, "Yeah, that works. The cep was a really good invention, Twinkaleni."

The mouse mage beams and they continue onward.

"Wow," blurts Danahlia as they finally make it to the small, rocky bottomed spring.

The water is clear and beautiful but the moist shore around it is crowded over with large, mostly brown and green jellies. The once thick grasses and shrubs around the spring are all dead or dying. Alice had never seen so many in one place before.

"They, they must be gorging themselves on the plants surrounding the spring," Twinkaleni offers in awe.

"If we take all these cores, we'll have plenty to trade with!" Alice says giving Danahlia the cep to draw her sword.

"We'll be able to get loads of food," the lizard girl practically drools.

"Hold on you two," Twinkaleni says grabbing hold of both of the larger girls' arms, "We've never faced so many at once. I believe some tact is an order."

The Murin mage has the trio follow a strict strategy in which the girls only engage lone jellies that have strayed from the groups along the shore. Though this method is a bit more rigid than they're used to, they do manage to collect many cores while reducing the jelly population swiftly, efficiently, and safely. The pixies are delighted at the dropping numbers and cheer the group on merrily from a safe height. But as they defeat jelly after jelly, the cep's jagged edge becomes steadily less effective.

Twinkaleni frowns at the end of the weapon, "It must be the corrosive effect of their slime. It's dissolving the shell. I'm afraid we won't be able to rely on this much longer."

"That's alright, we still have this," says Alice, brandishing her sword.

Danahlia adds, "We can make more. We still have some usable pieces from the crab."

Twinkaleni shakes her arms to let her long loose robe sleeves fall back, "Right, let us clear off the rest."

The girls fall back on their old strategy of Alice trading off her sword with Danahlia as Twinkaleni shifts each jelly's core off to the side with her magic, making it easier for the sword wielder to lop off that section.

After a consecutive series of battles, the few remaining jellies have drifted off, leaving the girls exhausted. Alice drops the last core onto the pile her shoulder bag had become buried under and collapses into the yellowing grass beside her friends.

She rolls to her back as Tally shouts, "Incredible you are! Defeated them all in a single day!"

The pixie lands on Alice's stomach, careful to avoid the goo stains all over her blouse, appearing to have tired herself with all her cheering. Danahlia and Twinkaleni are both laying back and breathing hard, but look over to the tiny figure.

"We *are* pretty incredible," Danahlia agrees.

"Truly you are the Jellybane," Shae praises happily as she joins her sister.

Alice grins at them, their weight slight even for their size.

"Did you have doubts?" Twinkaleni asks, still catching her breath.

"Gone now are all doubts, Master Orbear," assures the green haired pixie.

Tally suddenly grabs her sister's arm, "Tell the others the spring is safe once more we must!" Shae agrees and the pixies thank the girls for their efforts before flying off.

"Well, at least they're happy," Danahlia huffs, "Anyone bring anything to eat?"

Thinking their quest would be a short and easy one, they hadn't. Hungry and tired, the girls wash off some of the jelly from themselves and make their way back to camp, arms full of core stones.

It's evening by the time the weary trio arrive at their base. They have only the strength to dump there cores into a loose pile and flop down around the left over crab. They shove what they can into their mouths and groan each time one has to invest what's left of their flagging stamina to crack open another segment.

After supper, the girls lay in the grass until the sun begins to fall below the tree line. As the light fades, the glow from all the core stones brightens, keeping the ground around them lit. Each seems to have the intensity of a single candle, but together their light is magnified to the brightness of a small fire.

The girl's admire the wondrous glow for a time until Twinkaleni suggests they scatter them about the camp so even in total darkness, they can still see. The cores are placed in piles of four around the camp, and some even in low branches. The mostly brown and green glowing orbs illuminate the camp well enough for them to find their way around even as night closes in. With this last bit of work done, they climb up their tree and quickly fall asleep.

The next morning the trio wakes up late and sore when Danahlia shouts, "Hey! We're bein' raided!"

Alice rolls to her side to peer at the pointing lizard girl. Movement catches her eye and she looks below to more than a dozen giant gray ants roving over their supplies. Several of them are dragging away what's left of the crab. They've already taken the legs and claws. A group now attempts to lift away the body of the cooked crustacean.

"Ughey, hey! That's ours!" Alice grumbles as Danahalia leaps down among them.

The Liguna takes up her spear and begins stabbing and swinging at the six legged thieves. Alice grabs her sword to join her. The ants make no effort to defend themselves, instead completely focusing on stealing the girl's food. Even with her muscles burning, Alice chops and slices through them as she makes her way to the body of the crab being carried off by a handful of the massive insects. Just as she clears a path, a much larger ant snaps its long and horribly jagged mandibles at her leg causing the Tokala to stumble back and onto her butt. The giant among the giants closes in on her with frightening speed while Alice reaches blindly to her side for her weapon.

The monster's fearsome mandibles open wide to take Alice's foot just as Twinkaleni shouts, "Vespis flowmino!"

The goliath ant is hammered to the ground by a wind so powerful it blinds the fox as it disperses over her. Even so, the ant quickly attempts to get its many legs back under itself. It's nearly standing when Danahlia's spear impales its head, ceasing its movement instantly.

"That, my dear Alice, was a soldier," Danahlia huffs, leaving her spear in the monstrous ant to help the downed Tokala to her feet.

"Thanks," Alice says earnestly, retrieving her sword.

Danahlia smiles and then places her foot on the slain soldier's head to pull free her spear. Twinkaleni hurls down another burst of wind at the group taking the crab's body, sending the smaller ants flying in all direction, some even plopping into the stream. Without the help of their accomplices, the two remaining ants circle their prize uncertainly until Danahlia and Alice take them out. Those that are left scatter as Twinkaleni climbs down and Danahlia carries back the crab with Alice.

"Well, that's one way to wake up," Danahlia groans, letting her side of the crab drop.

Alice lets go of her side as well putting on a half smile, "At least we won't have to hunt for breakfast."

She shakes visibly as the adrenaline in her blood works its way through, grateful her friends were there to help when she needed it.

"Alice, are you alright?" Twinkaleni asks, planting her furless pink feet on the ground.

"Yeah, I'm ok," she answers, squatting in front of the imposing soldier ant.

"I'm just fine too, thanks for askin'," Danahlia assures them as she gathers a few of the more intact ants into a pile.

Twinkaleni gives the Liguna a look before stepping up beside the fox girl.

Alice smiles to Twinkaleni, "You guys really saved my tail."

"Of course we did," Twinkaleni grins back.

Danahlia's head pops up between them, her arms wrapping around both girls to pull them into a hug, "Yup, this is a good team to be on. Now, how's about we get a fire goin' and have us some ant."

"An excellent idea. I think the crab was beginning to turn in any case," Twinkaleni says, her large ears folding forward as she squeezes out of Danahlia's hold.

The girls gather up some fire wood and quickly get breakfast underway. While their ant is cooking, Alice pries off one of the soldier ant's forearm length mandibles. Using its jagged edge like a saw, she quite easily halves the crab's body. Popping it open causes a plume of fishy stink to flood out, forcing the young fox to turn away. She then slides it to the edge of the stream with her feet.

Alice briefly considers keeping the lower half to use as bait so they can possibly attract something else, but the powerful stench has her thinking better of it and she kicks it into the stream, letting it be carried away. She then cleans the top half out and fills it with water. She finds it does make a rather nice bowl, deep and sturdy. Emptying it and placing it on her head, she thinks, with a little cushion, it might make a nice helmet too.

"What are you doing?" asks Tally from behind.

Alice jumps a little but then poses for the pixie, "Tryin' on a hat. What do you think?"

"Most unusual," the pixie replies, with a tilt to her head.

Alice takes off the crab shell and sees Shae has also come, the green faye hovering around Twinkaleni as the Murin gathers the core stones that were scattered in the morning's battle.

Alice heads back to her friends, Tally following, and asks, "So were your friends happy to have the spring back?"

"Oh yes, brought you their thanks we have."

When Alice returns to camp, she notices several different types of birds fluttering about.

"Hey Alice, check it out," Danahlia calls excitedly, waving and pointing to a spot where the birds are landing briefly before taking off.

Each one of the birds has a tiny woven basket clutched in its beak and sets it down. Once the birds finish their work, they perch in the branches of the trees as if waiting for something. Danahlia crouches to pick up one of the baskets, small enough to fit in her palm, and dumps it to reveal a number of colorful grape-like berries. Alice joins her and empties another of the baskets, coming up with a small fruit similar in shape to a plum but aqua blue in color.

"Adonseea fruit and Jelessa berries," Tally supplies.

"Can we eat these?" Alice asks, watching Danahlia sniff the berries.

"Do, do," Tally encourages, "Picked this morning for the Jellybane and her friends they were."

"Wags," says Danahlia, putting down her basket to pop a berry into her mouth.

The moment her hand leaves the basket, one of the birds lands beside it, takes it in its beak by the tiny handle, and flies away.

As the girls watch it go, Danahlia comments, "Nice birds. Did you train them yourself?"

"Train we do not. The Chakor wish to show their thanks, ask us to lend our baskets they did."

"You can talk to birds?" Alice wonders.

"We mostly listen," the pixie replies.

Alice purses her lips curiously and then takes a bite from the blue adonseea fruit. As her sharp canine teeth pierce the delicate skin, a wonderful burst of sweet juice sprays her tongue. It's light and tangy, going wonderfully with the soft texture of the sun warmed flesh.

As she munches, Alice exclaims, "Wow, this is good."

Danahlia dumps her handful of berries into her mouth and chews them with gusto, "Mmm, where did you get these? I haven't seen any fruit trees around."

"From the Jelessa tree are those. Few there are now and carefully guarded are the ones that remain. Feed many they do," Tally explains.

"Why are there so few? Can't you plant more?" Alice asks, taking another bite of the succulent fruit.

"Once they were many, but the fallen fruit attracts the jellies. Too many to protect then. Now we gather all the fruit that falls and spread their seed in the hope that more will grow," Tally tells them somberly.

Twinkaleni approaches the small bundle of baskets with Shae, "So they take your water *and* food, another reason to rid the forest of these jelly monsters."

"Try these, Twinkie. They're great!" Danahlia encourages, handing her another basket of berries.

She does, and from her expression they must be delicious.

Danahlia grins and then asks the pixies, "Hey, do you guys know if there're any caves or something dry and large enough for us to sleep in?"

The pixies look to each other and Shae answers, "Many caves, but few are so large."

Alice continues listening while eating her fruit, delighted that rather than one large seed, it has many tiny ones that don't even need to be avoided.

"One close to a water source would be preferable if at all possible," Twinkaleni adds between berries.

As the pixies think on this, the scent of something burning reaches Alice's nose.

"Oh ticks, the ant!" Danahlia cries, rushing off to pull the blackening insect off the campfire.

"Well, we have plenty more, and thanks to our new friends, we even have fruit," Twinkaleni says happily, taking up an adonseea.

"Mm-hm," Alice agrees, trying the berries. She finds them to be sweet and juicy with a unique refreshing flavor that cools the mouth in the way that mint does.

Danahlia tosses the burnt ant aside and sets another to cook while the pixies hover high in whispered discussion. Twinkaleni notices the patiently waiting birds and dumps all the fruit into the crab shell bowl, letting the feathered animals take up their baskets to fly off in the same direction as the first. Alice watches them leave, curious as to where they're all going, but before she can ask, the pixies descend.

"A cave we know, suit you it might," Tally informs them.

"Though deep in the forest it is, a distance from here," adds Shae.

"A deeper location would help keep us hidden from anyone interested in looking for us, though it may also make it difficult to trade with the towns and villages around the edge of the forest," Twinkaleni considers aloud.

Alice looks to the pixies, "Is it safe there?"

They glance at each other and then Shae answers, "For the Jellybane, safe it may be."

Alice's eyebrow rises, "What does that mean?"

"The deep forest has long since been claimed by jellies, where they come from it is," Shae says as if it were common knowledge.

"More cores for us," Danahlia puts in, spinning the roasting ant over the fire.

"We'd be helping the pixies a lot if we cleared some out," Alice adds.

Tally blurts, "Help all you could! Benefit many it would."

"What would we do about clothes and things we can't get in the forest?" asks Twinkaleni, looking at her tattered, stained robe.

"We can always go feral," Danahlia chortles.

The girls discuss the matter over a nice breakfast of fresh fruit and barbecued ant. They offer some ant to the pixies, though they are hesitant to try it. Twinkaleni gives off a sort of check list of things they would need, while Danahlia, Alice, and the two pixies try to find solutions. They go over clothes and Danahlia feels confident that they can make leather clothes like hers from hides, Tally adding that the girls could also fashion things from leaves. Food is fairly plentiful in the forest if you know where and how to get it. The pixies offer their aid in this. When asked about water around the cave, the pixies hesitate. It turns out the two had only heard of it and have never actually seen it, though they claim to know right where it is, or is supposed to be.

Twinkaleni sighs, "I suppose we won't know if it will be large enough or protect us against the rain either until we see it for ourselves."

"A big cave it is said to be," Tally offers encouragingly.

"No offense to you or your people, Tally, but what seems big to you may be a bit small for all of us."

Danahlia claps her hands, "Whelp, looks like we're in for a hike."

"Even if it's not what we need, there are others, right?" Alice asks the pixies.

"Y-yes," Tally says, getting a look from her sister.

Alice furrows her brow at Danahlia, who shrugs.

Chapter 7

Taller

Decision made, the girls pack their things and leave the stream side camp for what they hope will be a nicer place to live. Shae has left the party leaving Tally to lead the girls, hovering a bit in front of them. Before leaving, they'd taken the other saw like mandible from the soldier ant as well as a few, but not all, of the core stones. Danahlia wanted to take them all but was out voted by the others, reasoning that they would only add to their weight and the trio would be getting more soon anyway. Danahlia also has most of one of the giant ants, insisting they should have it in case they can't find food. This turns out to be the least of their concerns, at least for Danahlia, who manages to find edible insects of various types to munch on as they walk.

Despite an already fairly slow pace, Tally begs the girls to defeat every stray jelly they encounter, claiming it's for the good of the forest and all who dwell within, save for the jellies apparently. They've gotten rather good at dispatching the lone monsters and work through them quickly.

Thanks to Tally and Shae's guidance, the sisters trading off every hour or so, the girls manage to travel between pools, ponds, and streams. This way they do not lack for water. Appreciative of their efforts, Alice, however, begins to feel a leading reason for the water hopping is to clear each spot of the inhabiting jellies for the pixies and their animal friends. This is further reinforced by the wild changes in direction the pixies insist on taking them.

The girls are on a break by one such pool when Twinkaleni informs them that they're being followed by an ever increasing number of the flying faye folk. Alice had noticed them too, though Danahlia, often at the front of the trio, seems to have been oblivious.

"Oh yeah, look," the Liguna calls, pointing them out. They hover in a tight group among the trees, staying a fair distance away. Their lights are all different colors, red, another pink, one silver, and a yellow. "Why don't they come over here?" Danahlia asks Shae, who is currently guiding the group.

"Young and nervous they are. The first taller they have seen are you," Shae explains.

Danahlia raises a brow, "Taller?"

"You and those like you. Varied you are, but all taller."

Danahlia grins at Twinkaleni, who holds herself up a little more, appearing quite proud to be considered a taller.

Tally returns to take over and the mouse mage gives the green haired pixie one of their core stones as she leaves. Alice watches the pixie take the stone in both slender arms, flying off through the small group of fairy lights. The pink one follows her.

"What'd you give Shae a core for?" wonders Alice.

"The pixies seem interested in the magic they contain. She said their elders might be able to use them," says Twinkaleni while Danahlia, a few yards away, waves at the other pixies.

Alice asks, "Use 'em how?"

"She mentioned binding, which is not a process I'm familiar with, but the way she described it, it sounds very similar to enchanting."

The curious Tokala's ears perk up, "What's that? Is it magic?"

"Of a sort, yes. Enchanting is the art of infusing mundane objects with energies to give them new properties."

The look on Alice's face must beg for Twinkaleni to continue because she grins as she does, "But unlike the magic I generally use, enchanting often involves an object with energy already contained within it be transferred to the object which is being enchanted."

"Like the core stones?" Alice asks, her eyes widening.

"Exactly. Perhaps the core stone's glow could be transferred to a common rock or maybe even a very durable bit of wood to make it glow as well." Alice's mouth steadily opens as Twinkaleni considers aloud, rubbing a large ear between two fingers, "Or perhaps even a core stone's glow could be transferred to another core to magnify the effect."

"Can you do that?"

"Oh, no. I read about the theory but I'm afraid I left the Order before I was taught to use it in practice," admits Twinkaleni.

Alice frowns looking to Danahlia, whose trying to coax the other pixies to come closer with Tally's help. Then she asks, "Why'd you leave?"

Twinkaleni's ears twitch, "The Order of Thermathrogi?" Alice nods as the pixies hover, hesitant to accept Danahlia's invitation. The mouse mage sighs heavily.

"You don't have to talk about it if you don't want to."

"It's alright. It might be nice to finally tell someone who will listen," she says, giving Danahlia a look as the Liguna waves at the red pixie. It flies away from the group, a little closer to her.

"Well, it was not an easy decision considering all that we had heard of the horrible things that would happen to us outside the walls of the Order."

As Twinkaleni goes on, Alice listens to how when the war had started, some of the more advanced mages were let out, which was never done. The younger magi left behind were told that those with the greatest control over their powers would serve in the army, and in so doing, would be given the chance to redeem themselves of their inherent evil. From then on, Twinkaleni and the others were taught about what was happening in the world. They were also made to study combat magic so they too may one day be allowed the privilege to serve. To the young magi who were continuously reminded of how foul and wicked they were for having the touch of magic, a chance for redemption was a reward they desperately sought. When Twinkaleni had reached a certain level of mastery with her evocation, she was allowed to train with other young magi.

Alice asks what evocation means and Twinkaleni replies, "It is the type of magic I most often employ, where energy is taken in, altered, and released, generally in a short burst."

"Like your wind spell?"

"Precisely. So as we trained, we were often paired with a partner to practice spells on. We would trade off, one attacking while the other would defend."

"You practiced on each other? That sounds dangerous."

"Quite so. We were taught to use the pain of our failure to improve. The incident that convinced me to leave the Order occurred during one such lesson. We where practicing fire magic and I was to attack while my..." Twinkaleni hesitates for a moment, "...opponent was to defend. My masters were watching and I wanted very much to impress them, so, I... struck," A deep frown appears as she shakes her head a bit, "His ward spell wasn't properly made and some of the heat bled through, burning him, rather severely." Alice listens enraptured as Twinkaleni stares wide eyed into some middle distance, "I was praised for this, for the pain I caused with my foolishness."

Alice watches the small mage for a moment and then asks, "What happened to him?"

The question seems to startle her and she looks up, "Oh, he tried to go on for a time despite his injuries, but was eventually deemed too damaged to continue. He was removed from the lessons and, I never saw him again. After that, I rather lost interest in the lessons myself. My masters noticed and informed me that if I did not improve, I would also be removed. Fearing what this might mean, I decided to escape."

"How'd you do that?"

"Well, with the fighting in the war intensifying, greater demand was made of the Order to produce powerful mages quickly. My masters would argue that to release a mage before being fully trained would be disastrous. Still, pressure was increased on the Order and new potentials were being rushed in as the more experienced magi were being sent out. With the increased traffic and chaos it brought, I managed to slip away."

Alice recalls Twinkaleni's nub of a tail and that she had mentioned losing it when she fled, so she asks about it.

"Mmm, while the Order's masters are not gifted in magic, they do possess many enchanted objects used to 'keep us in line' as it were. Once the alarm was raised after my absence was noticed, I imagine some great enchantment was used to erect the barrier that very nearly prevented my escape. I managed to cross before it reached its full power, though not without cost," she explains with a grim smile, feeling for the lost appendage.

Alice reaches out for the small girl, intent on giving her a hug but hesitates, her arms hanging in the air between them. Twinkaleni looks at her but doesn't recoil, so Alice moves in slowly until she can lightly put her arms around the mage. Twinkaleni lets her, the little Murin's shoulders steadily relaxing. Twinkaleni's light gray fur is incredibly soft and warm.

"I'm glad you made it out o' that place," Alice says honestly, while muzzling the back of one of Twinkaleni's large ears.

Alice is surprised to hear a sniff before she replies, "As am I."

Danahlia has managed to get the red pixie to hover around her while the others have come a little closer. The pixie has turned off its light and is revealed to be a boy with short fiery red hair, maybe a little more than half of Tally's height.

The red pixie's light flashes back on and he scrambles away when Danahlia rises to approach the hugging girls, "Hey, I could use a hug too."

Alice grins and lifts an inviting arm to her.

They all embrace for a comforting moment and with a last hard squeeze, Danahlia asks, "So, we ready to get goin'?"

The girls gather their gear and dawn their heavy packs, made heavier with their growing stash of core stones. As they walk, they discuss the lateness of the day and agree that they'll make camp for the night at the next water source. The other pixies follow close behind but seem to shy away from direct sight when Alice tries to look at them. Tally assures them that the girls will bring them no harm and they flutter a little closer. As they do, she has them to turn out their lights, which seems to require some effort on their part for the faces they're making when the young pixie's lights dim and their tiny forms come into view. The silver and yellow pixies turn out to be girls about the same size as the boy. One has two long pigtails of silver hair nearly as long as she is tall and the other has an intricate blonde braid down her back that drifts as she hovers about.

"I like your hair," says Alice.

They all say in subtly different high pitched voices, "Thank you," and then give each other looks.

"You are the Jellybane?" the silver haired one asks, fluttering closer.

"That's what your people call me."

"Big you are, but not as fearsome as I had thought," she admits.

Perhaps encouraged by the boldness of the other, the blonde haired one comes closer, "Soft your fur looks. Touch it may I?"

Alice grins, "Yeah, sure."

The finger sized pixie smiles brightly and flutters up somewhere above Alice. She can just feel a subtle warm current of air before the pixie lands on her head between her triangular fox ears.

"Oh, wondrously soft it is, Jellybane,"she exclaims and Alice can feel the slight girl's body moving around atop her head as if the pixie has lain down and is gathering up a bit of her fur in both tiny arms.

The other two pixies look to each other and then the red haired boy asks, "Touch it too may we?"

Alice laughs, "Sure."

The two pixies look delighted and quickly join their companion atop her head. Twinkaleni watches in amusement as they pet Alice's fur. One gets curious about her ears and it tickles when they touch one, making it twitch. She then feels wings and possibly hair as a pixie looks into it.

Disturbing the sensitive fluff there, Alice instinctively raises a hand to itch it with an annoyed, "Hey."

The pixies disperse, giggling, and fly away to pester Twinkaleni. The mouse mage is forced to raise the hood of her robe to keep them from probing and feeling around her own expansive ears. Danahlia laughs at the Murin's discomfort and the pixies move on to her next, feeling over her smooth skin. She waves her lengthy tail at them good-naturedly.

Alice is getting hungry and is relieved when Tally alerts them to their arrival at a small pond. The girls dump their gear in a pile and dispatch the few jellies that have congregated around the shore, the pixies cheering as they do. They then break for a few minutes before Twinkaleni begins filling waterskins, while Alice gathers wood for a fire, and Danahlia seeks a suitable tree for them to sleep in.

By the time Alice is returning to camp with an arm load of dry branches, Shae has returned with a scurry of over a dozen squirrels, all nearly double the size of any she had ever seen. Each carries a small pack on their backs. The chittering squirrels are mostly gray and brown with thick bushy tails. They wait patiently as the group of pixies removes their packs, which look to be woven from leaves and grass.

Alice sets down the wood she carries and then retrieves the crab shell bowl, setting it down beside the growing pile of tiny green backpacks. Twinkaleni and Danahlia start opening the packs, revealing more of the same ripe fruits and berries from the morning. They pile them into the bowl and the pixies return the packs to the squirrels. Each squirrel that receives their empty pack immediately scampers up a nearby tree. They then all head in the same direction back the way the girls had come, leaping from branch to branch to avoid the need to touch the ground.

"Where're they goin'?" Alice asks.

"The Salali go home. Return they will. Perhaps tomorrow, with more food for the Jellybane," Shae replies.

"Wags, can you thank them for us?"

Shae seems surprised by the request, "Made safer the forest is by your presence. They do this," she gestures to the fruit, "to thank *you*."

Tally gathers the smaller pixies, who have helped themselves to a few of the Jeleesa berries. Together with Shae they head off after the squirrels.

Tally calls back, "Return we will. Find your cave tomorrow, we might."

The girls wave to the fairies, their lights flickering on one at a time as they vanish into the forest. Alice is somewhat sad to see them go but her legs are tired and her stomach reminds her of other things. As they eat the succulent sweet fruit, Danahlia decides they should cook the thorax of the ant she's carried and save the abdomen for later. As the Liguna cooks, Twinkaleni settles down with two brown core stones.

Alice watches curiously and asks, "What're you gonna do with those?"

The Murin doesn't look up as she replies, "The conversation we had earlier has me considering the benefits of learning enchantment. I figure, we have plenty of cores, why not experiment a little? It may prove valuable."

With that the little mage closes her eyes and takes a deep breath. Alice takes this as a cue to be silent and observes. Twinkaleni keeps her tiny pink hands held out, one over each orb. Alice watches as the mage's breathing slows and her focus deepens.

After several minutes of unbroken concentration, Danahlia shouts, "TWINKIE!"

Both Alice and Twinkaleni jump, the little mage's eyes flashing open to glare at her reptilian friend.

Danahlia grins widely back, "How do you want your ant?"

"Danny!" Alice admonishes as Twinkaleni forces a deep breath, her little pink hands balling into fists, shaking angrily.

"What? I was just askin', geez," smirks Danahlia, returning her attention to the ant.

Twinkaleni settles down and once more closes her eyes. Danahlia turns to watch too, staying silent this time. Nothing happens for a while and Alice lays on her side, her head on her pack.

It's starting to get dark when Alice notices the glow from one of the core stones dimming while the others might be growing. The change is slight but in the fading day light, the one is definitely losing its glow. Twinkaleni's face is straining with concentration, her open hands flexing over both small spheres. Alice and Danahlia watch closely as the glow completely fades from one core stone while the other begins to vibrate while glowing brighter. Danahlia noses closer to the vibrating one and Alice picks up a faint hum that she's fairly sure is coming from it. The sound gets louder and Danahlia shares a questioning look with Alice who can only shrug.

Suddenly, with a terrible crackling pop, the brightening core stone explodes. Alice rolls away, covering her head, as Danahlia falls backward shouting in surprise and pain, leaving Twinkaleni gasping as if she had been holding her breath all this time. Alice thinks for a moment that the explosion is still going on until she realizes the sound reverberating in her ears is an echo from the surrounding forest. She turns back to find Twinkaleni heaving over Danahlia.

The Liguna is rolling on her back, holding her nose, crying, "Owww, ahh ticks, owww! Twinkie! What'd you do that for?! Ssss owww."

Trying to catch her breath, Twinkaleni huffs, "I'm so sorry, Danny. I... I didn't mean to, I swear. Here... let me see."

Alice crawls over to check on her as well. Danahlia tentatively removes her hands to reveal a vicious gash starting at her left nostril slit and traveling several inches along her muzzle. Blood oozes readily from the wound prompting Alice to quickly get water and a fresh blouse to clean it with. As she does, the Tokala notices movement in the crab shell bowl nearby. She glances over to it to find, beside a partially eaten berry, is the silver haired pixie girl. She sits up, seemingly dazed by the eruption of the core stone. She jumps when she realizes she's been spotted, her silver fairy light flickering on.

"What're you still doin' here? The others left a while ago," Alice informs the pixie while rummaging through her pack.

"Oh, gone with the others I should have, but curious I was about the Jellybane... and hungry," she admits, looking longingly at her half eaten berry.

"You should probably stay here with us," advises Alice, "The woods would be even more dangerous at night."

"Yes, Jellybane," she says obediently and flutters up out of the bowl. Flying around, she wonders, "Are there monsters? What made so horrible a noise?"

"It's Alice, and one of my friends is hurt," the Tokala answers, retrieving what she wanted and turning back to Danahlia. She pours a little water on a corner she makes with her blouse, kneeling beside the wounded girl to wipe away the blood.

Danahlia winces at her touch, "Easy! That hurts!"

"Sorry, but I have to clean it or it might get worse," insists Alice.

The Liguna endures her touch while Twinkaleni looks on, apologizing over and over.

"Cut it out, Twinkie. I know you didn't mean it," Danahlia mumbles and then hisses as Alice runs the freshly dampened cloth over the wound once more.

"Help I can," the little silver haired pixie announces, fluttering over Danahlia's nose.

"That's ok, firefly, I think we got it," the Liguna grumbles, blowing a little air at her.

The pixie swirls in the updraft and cries out, "Airiliantachu, and mend I can!"

"Bless you. Seriously, we're good, and your light's makin' me feel nauseous."

Alice watches as the silver light shakes a bit and, with a little grunt of effort, goes out.

The pixie lets out a breath before saying, "Apologies, Devourer, but mend you I can, watch and see."

Danahlia looks up at her, "What did you call me?"

"Quite, Danny. This could be very educational," Twinkaleni chides, then gives the pixie an encouraging, "Go on, little one."

Danahlia settles down and lets the slight, silver haired pixie land on her nose. Just as the others, her skin is so pale it nearly seems to glow on it's own and all she wears are a few well-placed leaves. She has large silver eyes and is very beautiful. The pixie kneels at Danahlia's cut nostril and as she waves her hands over the wound, she begins to sing of all things. Alice doesn't understand the words but finds them to be soothing. They watch the pixie sing her song, her arms gently waving in the air as if on a breeze, mesmerized by her tune and graceful movements.

By the time Airiliantachu finishes, both Twinkaleni and Alice have leaned in so close that they bump into each other as they pull away. The pixie takes to the air and Danahlia rubs her nose curiously. Alice and Twinkaleni look from the pixie to see there isn't even a scar left.

"How's it look? Am I still pretty?" Danahlia asks.

"As you ever were," Twinkaleni smirks, making Danahlia grin.

"That was amazing, Airlyachu," Alice says feeling over Danahlia's unmarred flesh.

"Airi...lianta...chu...," the pixie corrects in a drained tone, dipping in the air.

Danahlia reaches for the pixie just as she begins to fall, catching the tiny girl in her palm. The girls crowd their faces around the slender pixie, who appears utterly exhausted.

"That healing song must have worn her out," Alice observes, as the pixie lays flat in Danahlia's hand.

"It is no wonder. The complexity of healing magic is magnitudes greater than anything I can achieve. From what I've read, even among those gifted with magic, few can ever hope to learn such skill," Twinkaleni remarks, "Most healers must be born with an aptitude for it."

"I'm keepin' you with me," Danahlia asserts to the passed out pixie.

She then takes Alice's blouse, turning it to a clean side and places it in the crab shell bowl with what remains of their fruit. Once she does, she places the silver tressed pixie onto the makeshift bed and checks on the cooking ant. Announcing that it's ready, the girls gather around while Danahlia breaks it open with a stick. The legs got a little burnt but the ant's gooey insides smell just as delicious as the first time Alice had tried it.

Twinkaleni looks over to her failed attempt at enchanting. The core she intended to strip of its glow has become black and brittle while the other was completely destroyed. Alice waits for the ant to cool some and pokes at the blackened core. It collapses into a pile of ash like dust.

"I'm so sorry Danny. I hope you know I'd never use my magic to cause you any harm," Twinkaleni professes.

"Pshh, I know that, Twinkie. What were you tryin' ta do anyway?" the Liguna replies with a negligent wave of her hand.

"I was attempting to infuse one core with another's glow to make it brighter. I thought it might work better as a light source," the Murin explains.

Danahlia tilts her head a little, "I didn't know you could do that."

Twinkaleni's ears droop, "Clearly, I cannot."

"I think you almost had it," says Alice encouragingly, "I saw the one core's glow dim and the other's strengthening, just before it…"

"Yeah, I did too. It almost worked," Danahlia adds, nodding.

Twinkaleni shakes her head grimly, "I don't think it would be wise to try again."

"You gotta try again!" insists Danahlia, "If we can trade regular cores for a decent amount, super bright glowin' cores have to be worth way more! Think of all the food we could buy!"

Twinkaleni frowns a little and Alice adds, "We can take precautions. Maybe do it behind a tree or somewhere to keep the pieces from flying all over if it pops again."

Twinkaleni's jaw clenches before she says, "I don't know. What if someone was hurt? That shard could have easily taken your eye, Danny."

"Then we do like Alice said, make a safe place. And we won't sit around gawkin'," assures Danahlia.

"Yeah, you can do it, Twinkaleni. We believe in you," Alice encourages.

"Enchanting would be an valuable skill," the Murin admits, warming to the idea.

The girls discuss the possibilities while they have their giant ant. Danahlia continuously reminds them of the good food they could buy. Alice is more interested in what magical items Twinkaleni might be able to make. They also go over how core stones with a brighter glow would be wonderful for lighting their cave, assuming it was serviceable. Twinkaleni tries not to get their hopes too high, insisting that it may take many trials to get even the core stones to work properly, but agrees it will be worth the effort.

After eating so much fruit, they're stuffed before finishing most of the ant and it's gotten dark. Rather than set up Alice's tent, the girls take their time, carefully bringing their gear up with them into a large nearby oak. Danahlia manages to carry Twinkaleni on her back with her tail wrapped around the crab shell bowl, Airiliantachu still slumbering within. Exhausted from their journey they quickly fall asleep.

The next morning is lively. Tally, Shae, and the pixie children have returned, along with several new comers. They also brought an assortment of their fruit carrying, feral friends. Airiliantachu has recovered and is severely scolded by Shae for having not returned with the others. The silver haired pixie apologizes profusely while enduring angry shouts about how the others had searched the forest for hours despite the dangers of darkness, fearing the worst. Shae demands she returns home with her but Danahlia insists she can stay if she wants to. The little pixie does and Shae drops it, but only because the Devourer requests it.

The pixies have brought a number of ferals this time. Some of the new ones vaguely resemble the large squirrels but with leaf shaped ears, long furred tails, and a thin skin that extends from their forelimbs to their hinds. Each of these has a small spherical gourd loosely hanging around their necks. When asked what they are, Tally tells them that they are called, Aludi.

Danahlia takes up one of the gourds, asking, "Can we eat these?"

Tally points to a tiny cork made of folded leaves on one end of the gourd, "Oh no, Devourer, contain the nectar of the Niurha tree they do. You are meant to drink it."

As Danahlia pulls the cork free, she asks, "You guys keep callin' me, Devourer. What's that about?"

Tally seems hesitant but answers, "Consumed many things you have since entering the forest. Many things we do not eat, like the biters, the spinners, the crawlers, and even the great clawed one." She points to their crab shell bowl.

Danahlia purses her lips and considers. "Mmm, Devourer, I kinda like it. I am the Devourer, eater of things!" she announces proudly, which startles the new pixies into huddling together into a ball of multicolored light.

Alice grins and uncorks another of the gourds, sniffing its contents. The scent is subtle while fruity.

"Please drink, Jellybane. Restore your strength it will," Tally encourages.

Alice covers the little hole with her lips and tilts the gourd until a wondrously flavorful, sweet liquid graces her tongue. It's thin like water but has a unique flavor that immediately brings to mind images of fresh growth in the forest after a long awaited rain. Too soon the palm-able gourd is empty and she tries to stick her tongue in it to get any remaining drops.

Twinkaleni joins them after fending off the pixie children, her hood over her ears, as Danahlia asks, "That good huh?" Alice, now sucking on the gourd, 'mm-hm's enthusiastically and Danahlia downs her nectar, nodding her approval, "Mmm, not bad. Try it Twinkie."

The Murin mage takes up a gourd for herself and has a sip, then drains it, commenting when she finishes, "Ah, most refreshing. Where did you get this?"

Tally bobs up and down happily, "Nectar from the Niurha tree. A rarely blooming tree it is but eagerly wait we do. Please drink all you wish. Need your strength today you will. The cave awaits."

The girls eagerly drink their share of three gourds each. As they finish each one, the pixies tie them back onto the long tailed Aludi. The moment they're set, the creatures scurry up the nearest tree and then, to Alice's amazement, leap, spreading their limbs and gliding on their thin skin flaps from trunk to trunk until they're out of sight, Shae and some of the new pixies following them. The girls then dine on the fruit, brought by birds and the large squirrels. As Alice eats, she notices the weariness of the last few days slipping away to be replaced with new strength. Her muscles steadily ache less and soon her entire body feels invigorated.

"Wow, I feel great!" she bursts.

Danahlia nods, fruit juices dripping down her chin, "Yeah, me too."

"Mmm, indeed. It's as if my body is being rejuvenated," says Twinkaleni, looking over herself in amazement.

Tally bobs excitedly in the air, "The Niurha's nectar it is! Renews the body it does."

"That reminds me, did you know the silver haired pixie can heal injuries?" Alice asks, suddenly feeling better than she had in a long time.

"Airi? Yes. Precious is her gift. Frightened of losing her we all were."

"Are there other pixies that can use such magic?" Twinkaleni asks.

"Mmm, gifts we all have," says Tally, "but rarest are those who can mend. Only one is Airi."

"What's your talent?" Danahlia wonders, munching on some fruit.

Tally spirals, "Find things I can."

The girls begin gathering their possessions after they finish their breakfast and make ready for another hike. Energized and even excited, the girls continue to ask Tally questions as they depart and begin walking. The pixie reveals that all her kind have special gifts or abilities. Tally is especially good at finding things, even in the dense forest. Because of this, she was more or less chosen to follow the Jellybane and then to lead her and her friends about. Tally assures them, unconvincingly, that the fact they were hitting areas with large concentrations of jellies was just a 'most fortunate coincidence.'

The small party ventures on much as they had yesterday, heading from water source to water source, disposing of the jellies congregating there, and collecting their cores. It gets to the point that they have so many the girls purposely leave the less valuable ones behind. After each battle they take a break, noticing almost every time they do, Shae and Tally switch places to lead the girls while a few more pixies accompany them. The new ones sometimes hover around to look at the 'taller' but their primary reason for coming seems to be taking the discarded cores back to wherever the tiny beings keep coming from.

"What are you guys doin' with those cores?" Alice asks Shae, pointing to a purple pixie carrying one off.

"Power they have. Use it we can," she replies.

"How'd you do that?"

"Oh, not I, the elders. How, I know not. Told to collect them we were."

As they continue on, the other young pixies are ushered away but Airi insists on staying, and with Danahlia backing her, Tally and Shae give up on trying to take the healer home. From her they learn more about the pixies and their struggle with the jellies. Like Airi, other pixies have magic too. Some can even use spells like Twinkaleni to fight but it takes many of them working together to have much effect. Because of this, the pixies can only protect a few key areas, such as their precious fruit trees, around which they and their animal friends tend to live. Airi expresses great hope and gratitude for Alice and her friends, who defeat the jellies with incredible ease.

By late afternoon, the rejuvenating effect of the Niurha nectar is long gone and the girls are sagging under the ever increasing weight of their packs. Not for the first time, Alice wonders if they're close to the cave and again Tally bobs, claiming they are. Shae appears from the direction the group is headed and reveals that the cave is just ahead. Relieved, the girls slog the rest of the way, eager for the days march to be over with.

The green haired pixie had been scouting ahead and reports that some weavers have claimed the cave they were seeking.

"What're weavers?" Danahlia asks.

"Spiders," Alice clarifies, "Big ones."

Twinkaleni stops, "Uh, I'm afraid I am not terribly fond of spiders."

"That's ok, me and Alice can handle 'em," Danahlia assures her. An idea Alice is not terribly fond of.

"How big and how many are there?" Alice asks Shae.

"Apologies, Jellybane, only the weaver's silk I saw," the little pixie admits, which makes Alice even less enthusiastic.

They come to a cliff side maybe thirty feet high and Shae instructs them to follow her. Moving along the rocky wall, the girls eventually find a slim opening with thick spider's web all over the walls, floor, and ceiling. It clings to all the stone surfaces, disappearing into the darkness within.

"What'd you think, Twinkie?" Danahlia asks, as she and Alice peer into the cave mouth to no reply. "Twinkie?"

They look back to see Twinkaleni still a dozen yards back with Tally and Airi hovering overhead.

Alice looks up to Shae, "Are you sure this is the right cave?"

"No other there is," the pixie replies, fluttering back and forth nervously.

Danahlia waves for Twinkaleni to come to her but the Murin shakes her head, "I don't like spiders, especially big ones."

"Nor I!" Tally is quick to add.

Danahlia sighs to Alice, "I guess it's just us then."

"Is this a bad time to tell you I don't like spiders either?" Alice groans, looking into the foreboding slit in the rocks.

Danahlia places a hand on the Tokala's shoulder, "Too late. So how'd you wanna do this?"

In truth, Alice would rather not 'do this' at all, but if they had to, she suggests they try to lure any spiders out into the open rather than try to fight them in the tight dark passage.

Danahlia nods, "Yeah, that's what I was thinkin'. But we'll need bait."

Hearing this, Shae stiffen and then tries to flee but with lightning reflexes, Danahlia extends out her tail ahead of her and the pixie runs right into it.

Danahlia catches the dazed pixie as she pleas, "No, Jellybane, do this not! Eat our kind weavers do!"

"Calm down, Shae, we won't let anything happen to you. We have a plan," Alice assures as the diminutive figure struggles in Danahalia's grip. She looks to the lizard girl, "Right?"

"Course I have a plan," Danahlia states, "sort of."

Chapter 8

The Cave

The plan has Shae squirming against the web just inside the cave, crying to be let go. Danahlia has the tiny faye wrapped in her tail and a bit of silk to keep her in place while the Liguna and Tokala wait in ambush on opposite sides of the cave's mouth.

"Please, do not let my sister be eaten," Tally begs, hovering in circles over Danahlia's head.

Twinkaleni and Airi have come closer as well but keep a safe distance.

"Don't worry, I'll pull her out before that ever happens," Danahalia assures Tally, taking a firm two handed grip on her spear, then she calls, "Tell us when you see somethin', Shae."

"Release me, please! Do this not! Another way there must be!" the captive pixie cries.

Over the pixie's wailing, Alice can just make out a rapid clicking noise, one that steadily gets louder. She gives Danahlia a look and the Liguna nods. Alice grips her freed sword harder.

"Coming they are! Please, let me go!" Shae cries in panic.

She then lets out a terrified, high pitched scream and Danahalia shouts, "NOW!"

In the span of a heartbeat, Danahlia pulls her tail and the pixie free as both armed girls thrust their weapons into the cave, Danahlia aiming high while Alice strikes low. Danahlia manages to skewer a massive spider right in its mouth, the thing dropping from the wall where it was crawling. Alice comes up short but isn't off by much as a handful of the unsettlingly large arachnids come boiling out toward them.

A breath catches in Alice's throat as Danahlia screeches, "Oh, Ticks!" when they see their numbers, both girls falling back.

They're just as large as the lone spider Alice had freed Tally from a few days ago. Though these are covered with coarse gray, black, and yellow hairs that make them look ferociously thorned. As the monsters approach, they click their fangs together in a menacing chorus, their eight slender legs carrying them forth with surprising speed.

Alice panics, trips over a stone, and lands hard on her back. Danahlia manages to leap away, swinging her spear to fling the first impaled monstrosity off while managing to beat back another against the rocks. She spins to slam her tail into it sending the arachnid flying back with Shae screaming in terror, still stuck to the Liguna's lengthy appendage with thick sticky threads of silk.

One of the spiders leaps with unexpected agility and nearly lands on Alice's face, only to be bisected into two uneven parts by the Tokala's sword, warm ichor falling over her. She scrambles to get to her feet and slashes at another as it approaches, taking off its front legs. As the spider falls forward into the dirt, Alice chops down hard on its head, causing the remaining flailing limbs to go limp instantly. Danahlia misses with a thrust but manages to knock another spider away with the butt of her spear. As it recovers, it's joined by two more, one leaping at her face. Danahlia manages to impale the leaper but is left open to the last two. Knowing she won't make it in time, Alice hurls her sword at the advancing horrors, but the blade flies well over them.

The monsters are only feet away, fangs clicking eagerly, when Twinkaleni calls, "Feasta!"

A small stream of fire washes over the spiders from the side, setting their hairy bodies aflame. Danahlia has to dodge them as they frenzy, fleeing a short distance before collapsing into burning heaps. Alice lets out the breath she feels like she'd been holding the entire battle, recovering her sword on wobbly legs. Danahlia flings the still wiggling spider from her spear, finishing it off where it lands before pulling a shivering Shae from the end of her tail. She, with Tally, then tries to pull the webbing off the petrified pixie. Twinkaleni approaches while Alice inspects the cave, listening for any more clicks.

"Nice shot, Twinkie," Danahlia grins.

Twinkaleni nods, taking in deep breaths, watching the flaming spiders go out. Danahlia puts the violently shaking Shae on the ground, leaving the delicate work of removing the remaining web to her sister and Airi. She then checks the spiders to make sure they remain still.

"Are there any more?" Twinkaleni asks.

Alice, angling her ears by the cave mouth, shakes her head, "I don't think so. At least I don't hear any." The sun is going down and the distance Alice can see into the cave diminishes with it. "What should we do?"

"Estraleete," Twinkaleni murmurs.

A ball of light the color and brightness of a candle's flame appears between her hands. She sends it into the cave with a little pushing gesture, illuminating the cramped passage's inners. Web coats everything but fortunately doesn't span across the passage, though a curve keeps them from seeing further. The magic light pops silently out of existence when it hits the bend.

"It seems we will have to go in if we wish to see more," Twinkaleni says regretfully.

Alice frowns at the prospect. Tally has managed to get her sister unstuck enough to fly. She tells them they will return and then flutters off, her and Airi helping Shae along.

Danahlia joins the others at the mouth of the cave, "So, we goin' in or what?"

"Sure, you first," Alice bows graciously.

Danahlia snorts, "Fine. Twinkie, a light if you please."

The Murin mage creates another little ball of orange light and the trio move in. Danahlia leads, her spear held before her, with Alice following. Twinkaleni brings up the rear, trying to hold the light high over her head in an effort to let it shine over the taller girl's shoulders. The cave forces them to walk single file, and even doing so they still brush against the thick sticky web on the sides. Though, at the very least, it's tall enough that they don't have to hunch.

It's dry and dusty inside. Just as they pass the curve a few yards in, Twinkaleni sneezes. The girls jump at the sound and the light goes out, plunging them into pitch blackness. Danahlia back pedals into Alice, the butt of her spear poking the fox girl in the ribs as she calls nervously, "Twinkie, light."

The mouse mage sniffs and then uses her spell again. Only a few feet after the curve the cave opens into a decent sized chamber. There are several silk wrapped bundles around and no visible passages out which leads the group to believe that this must have been where the spiders had been nesting.

Twinkaleni warns that she can't keep the light going much longer and seeing no visible threat, they make their way back out. It's getting dark now and the girls gather there things to take into the cave. They each grab a handful of glowing core stones from their stores, placing them in crevices, rock shelves, the floor, anywhere that can support them to help light the passage. They then spread more cores all over the main chamber, managing to get much of it lit, if only dimly. By then they're all very hungry and tired but without firewood they can't cook their last ant segment.

For now, they clear a spot on the ground, pushing whatever unfortunate creatures are wrapped inside the web cocoons off to the side and into a pile. The space isn't large but the girls do what they can to settle in, Alice using her pack and some of Danahlia's lengthy tail as a pillow. Twinkaleni seems hesitant to join them in such a confined space.

Danahlia claps her hands and holds them out to the Murin, "Come on, Twinkie, get in here."

The mouse mage sighs but joins them on the floor and Alice gives her a companionable rub along her arm while Danahlia roughly pets her head. Hungry but warm among her friends, Alice eventually drifts off to the sound of rumbling bellies.

In the darkness, Alice hears the menacing clicks of another large spider. Pixie lights come on in a ring around the cavern and she finds herself on the floor, alone. The lights chant in dozens of ugly little voices, "Je-lly-bane, Je-lly-bane, Je-lly-bane." The clicks get louder and she turns to the only way out but freezes as a massive spider, far larger than all the others combined, makes its way in, blocking the exit. Its fangs click together, dripping transparent green venom, its many eyes glowing red with vengeance. Alice scoots back on her rump until her back is against the far wall, her mouth open in wordless fear. The spider pulls its enormous body into the small chamber, all the while the pixies continue to chant, "Je-lly-bane, Je-lly-bane, Je-lly-bane." The spider clicks its fangs at her, closing the distance in a second, it's two front legs poised for the attack.

Defenseless, Alice tucks into a ball, raising her arms over her face, not wanting to see death coming. The moment she feels the moist warmth of the monster's breath she screams, kicking out with both legs.

The spider lets out a pained, "Ow!" then it's gone and Alice sees the cave isn't lit with pixies but the glowing core stones.

"What the tick, Alice?!" Danahlia grumbles angrily.

"Are you alright?" Twinkaleni appears before her, large ears and concerned face blocking out most of the chamber.

Alice takes a few calming breaths, her skin tingling with goosebumps, "Yeah, yeah, just a bad dream." But she still hears someone calling, "Jellybane, Jellybane."

"Sounds like Tally's back," grumbles Danahlia, rubbing a spot on her thigh. Alice offers apology as the girls stretch and then head out to meet their winged friend.

The pixie hovers in front of the cave mouth and bobs excitedly when she sees them, "Stay you did, good. Worried I was. Come, come, brought much we have!"

The girls squint into the early day, greeted by another gathering of assorted animals, all bearing packs of some sort, and even more pixies. The pixies have already begun relieving their feral companions of their supplies, putting them into a growing pile.

"Wags, I was starvin'!" Danahlia cheers and starts unwrapping fruit to stuff into her mouth. The pixies avoid her then, putting the small packs of fruit into a new pile.

Alice marvels at the variety of animals that showed up this time. Various birds, small mammals, and some more creatures she doesn't recognize at all watch the girls, mostly from the safety of trees. One sort has very long arms and short legs with several grasping fingers ending each limb. It has white fur and large eyes with a fairly small body. As the packs are removed by the pixies from its kind, the creatures quite easily scale a nearby tree and wait patiently to have their emptied packs returned to them.

Joining her friends to a feast of colorful fruits, Alice asks about the assembled creatures. Tally tells her that most of them used to live in and around the areas the girls have been clearing and eagerly await the day they can return to their homes. She feels terribly guilty when the pixie informs her that the fruit she and her friends were eating so gluttonously had often come from the ferals own rations, but that they were more than willing to give it if it meant the forest would be made safe for them again.

Alice tries offering some of the fruit to the gathered animals, which only look at her curiously.

Tally interjects, "No Jellybane, keep your strength up you must. Worry not, fed they will be once they return."

She watches the animals immediately depart the moment their packs are given back to them and tries to savor each bite of their sacrifice. Twinkaleni slows in her eating as well, though Danahlia seems unaffected by the news.

They both look at her and she looks back, "What? We're helpin' 'em so they're helpin' us." The two stare at her some more. "We earned this," Danahlia argues, waving an adonseea fruit. The fox and mouse girls frown at her. "Tally said it was ok," she reasons and they keep it up. "Ugh, what do you want me to do?"

"I think we should save some, you know, try to make it last," Alice suggests.

"I agree. If we limit our intake to necessity, perhaps the pixies and their friends will not feel they need to give more," Twinkaleni adds.

Danahlia groans, "Fine," and she shakes the fruit again, "Can I eat this or are you two gonna keep givin' me that look?"

The girls finish their meal, sure to make a show of putting some aside for later. Once all the animals depart with their empty packs, the pixies hover around the caves. Alice wonders what they're doing until she sees them taking bundles of silk in their arms before flying away. She asks Tally about this and the pixie says they can make things from the weaver's threads.

After breakfast, efforts are made to clean up their new home. Spider silk and the wrapped bundles are left out for the pixies that periodically return to gather them up. Once that's done, Danahlia and Alice wait outside while Twinkaleni generates an impressive gust from within the cave, blowing out a great deal of dust and debris. The Murin mage emerges, coughing, but the cavern is made all the nicer for her efforts. Core stones are replaced and added to which helps brighten the interior even more. Twinkaleni has them build a short wall at the entrance from stones to keep jellies and other things out. It's just tall enough that even the mouse girl can hop over it. Tally then takes them to a nearby spring where they can get water and wash off.

The spring is guarded by various jellies, some even the prized red. The girls clear it, adding the cores to their swelling hoard before making use of the cool clean waters. The rest of the day is spent near camp. Alice collects fire wood for a time, while Danahlia scouts out the surrounding area with Airi, and Twinkaleni remains near the cave with Tally. First the mouse mage uses some water to make mud. With it, she packs the little wall at the cave entrance to make it more stable. She then discovers a crevice nearby, in front of which she makes another stone wall. When Alice returns, dumping an arm load of sticks and branches, she asks the Murin what she's doing.

"I'm going to give enchanting another try. I believe this will help keep collateral damage to a minimum," says Twinkaleni, putting the finishing touches on her barrier.

"Wags, mind if I watch?" Alice asks.

"Oh, if you wish," Twinkaleni says a bit nervously, "Though I must ask you do so from a distance. I'd hate for you to get hurt."

The curious Tokala settles in a ways off to the mage's side, Tally landing atop her head, as

Twinkaleni sets two core stones in the crevice behind her little wall. She sits down on the opposite side, her barrier just tall enough that she can see over it if she leans while still offering her body protection. Twinkaleni extends her arms around either side of the barrier, her hands open and palms toward the cores. Alice can't see very well, and waits, watching the Murin mage's concentration deepen over the next several minutes.

Twinkaleni's expression becomes steadily more strained until Alice jumps at the sound of another exploding core. Twinkaleni cries out, holding one of her large ears.

Alice leaps to her feet, Tally grabbing some of her fur to hold on as she runs to her friend, "Are you alright?"

Twinkaleni groans in irritation, "Fine. A shard hit my ear is all."

Alice kneels beside her to check and finds a little blood amidst the delicate pink flesh of mouse mage's inner ear. Having nothing else at hand to offer, Alice licks the wound clean.

Twinkaleni shudders in surprise, "What are you doing?"

"You're bleedin'," Alice informs between licks.

"Oh, is it bad?"

"No, it's just a little," says Alice, finishing.

"Uh, well... thank you," Twinkaleni smiles.

Alice gets an idea and rushes off to gather some large leaves. She makes a bed of them and then dumps their small store of fruit out upon it from the crab shell bowl. She then brings the bowl to Twinkaleni, who's replaced the ruined cores with two new ones, both green, and sits to try again. Alice places the bowl atop the mage's head. Twinkaleni shies away from it, but Alice insists it will help, so the Murin mage lets her. Alice folds back both of Twinkaleni's large flexible ears so they wrap almost to the back of her head and fits the bowl on to keep them there.

The little mouse gives her a questioning look and Alice grins giving the makeshift helmet a tap. It's much too big and she looks silly but unbelievably cute as she goes on to try enchanting again.

Tally flutters around Alice's head as the Tokala settles back in to watch, "Clever you are, Jellybane. Difficult is the gifted one's challenge."

"Do you know how to enchant things?" Alice wonders of the blue haired pixie as she perches on her head once more.

Tally doesn't but says she knows some of her own kind that do and through them, knows of its complexity. Alice asks about Shae, who hadn't reappeared since the battle with the spiders yesterday. Tally says her sister is well and resting after the ordeal, though she may make an appearance later. Talk turns to the jellies as they watch Twinkaleni.

Currently, they are near the heart of the forest, where the jellies are the most concentrated. Tally informs the hunter that there are many spots in this general area where the jellies tend to congregate and would very much like for Alice and her companions to clear them. They're discussing plans to do so in the next few days when Twinkaleni pops another core.

They both jump as Twinkaleni ducks behind her wall, a piece pinging off the crab shell helmet. Not hurt this time, the mouse mage smiles and gives

Alice a thumbs up before she replaces the ruined cores with two more from the pack at her side.

A piece of core falls near Alice and Tally flutters over to grab it, "Have this can I?" she asks.

"Uh, yeah sure," Alice nods. The pixie grins widely before flying off into the forest.

"Hey guys! Check it out!" Danahlia calls, returning to camp with Airi.

The Liguna has something slung over her shoulder and swings it around to drop it on the ground. It's a very large lizard of some kind. The body alone is over two feet long and the lengthy tail several more.

Alice and Twinkaleni approach her, Alice asking, "What is that?"

"Meat," Danahlia says proudly.

"A spitter it is," adds Airi.

"You want to consume this? Are you sure it's edible?" Twinkaleni asks, looking over the reptile.

Danahlia points and laughs at the Murin, "Why's that on your head?"

Twinkaleni feels up at her crab shell helm self-consciously, "It's proven quite useful."

Danahlia gets some more laughs in making Twinkaleni narrow her eyes at her before the girls turn their attention to the slain lizard creature. Danahlia insists it can be eaten but Alice and Twinkaleni consult the young pixie to be sure. She says it's not poisonous and when asked about its name, Danahlia recounts it spitting a glob of sticky saliva at her. Airi has heard that if small ferals are hit with this projectile it can pin them to a surface and even make it impossible for pixies to fly, turning either into an easy meal. She notes that this one is a younger spitter and despite occasionally eating pixies, shows remorse for the lost life.

While the girls discuss what is to be done with the spitter, Alice gets a good look at its features. The lizard is long and slim with fairly short limbs, each tipped with curved claws making her think it would easily scale trees. It has a pointed head that widens like an arrow and a lengthy tapering tail. Its skin is smooth and grass green with bright yellow stripes running the length of its body. Danahlia must have caught it with the tip of her spear, for the large bleeding hole just under its right forelimb.

The Liguna decides to skin it for the hide, but finds this a difficult, messy, and smelly task as she works with the saw like soldier ant mandibles collected earlier. She eventually gives up and simply cuts the creature into bits to set over a fire made by Alice and Twinkaleni. By then its evening and Tally has gone to see if any of her animal friends want to visit the Jellybane's camp. Several ferals and fairies return with her just as the lizard is finished cooking and the girls have a feast of fruit and meat.

More pixies than animals come this time. Some helping their feral friends unload fruit and reload with cores but most simply hover around the camp talking among themselves. A few of the braver ones come closer for short periods but always flutter back to their colorfully lit little groups. Tally says most of them are younger pixies, curious about the Jellybane and her companions. They seem very amused when Danahlia tries the lizard for the first time, pointing and giggling. Danahlia raises a brow to them curiously before resuming her bite.

She chews in thought for a moment before approvingly commenting, "Not bad." And so Twinkaleni and Alice try some.

The skin is still on for the most part and has become thin, flaky, and has little flavor. Alice finds the meat to be rather nice, tasting faintly of wood smoke more than anything else, but it's warm and filling. Along with the sweet fruit, it is a very nice meal. While they eat, Tally gets a few of the pixies to start singing, and as they sing they dance.

Like Airi's, this song is in a language the girls don't understand but it has a nice uplifting melody. They watch the pixies fly around each other in intricate patterns, their lights flashing in sync with their words to create quite a show. Danahlia starts to put her own words to the pixies' tune.

"See the lights floating in the trees? Twirlin' and flippin' all on a breeze," she sings and then leans into Twinkaleni, nudging the smaller girl with an elbow, "You're seein' this right, Twinkie?"

The mouse mage shoves the larger girl away with both hands before being able to resume watching the display.

Smiling, Danahlia starts with a heavier beat in her voice, "Follow the greens and the blues and the reds, flashin' and dippin' all around our heads. Blink even once and you might miss your chance, to see the magic of the pixie's dance."

Nodding along Alice adds, "Even in the dark of the night, together they make the woods so bright. Yellows and purples and pinks all around, isn't it wonderful what we've found."

The two girls add lines when they can think of them and Twinkaleni hums with the tune, grinning as the pixies flutter about, adopting the new words with remarkable ease.

Once the song ends, the pixies let out a joyous cheer. They lose their previous hesitation and swarm over the girls, laughing merrily while singing parts of the song. Tally calls to them good-naturedly to turn off their lights but in all the excitement only a few listen. Alice closes her eyes against the dizzying array of colors, laughing as dozens of tiny hands pet and feel her fur. They land atop her head and arms, running their delicate limbs through her sunset orange coat. Some feel around her ears causing them to flick, which only encourages the delighted pixies on. A few get curious about her teeth and she can feel them reaching in to touch her canines. Alice gives them a little blow, sending pixies spiraling and giggling away.

The girls only endure this for a minute or two before Tally and some of the older pixies start getting them together to leave for the night. The young pixies let out a chorus of *oh*s and *aww*s as they gather together into a cloud of multicolored lights. Some linger, getting a last look or feel of fur before joining the rest, while others have to be escorted. Eventually the pixies depart, leaving Alice and Twinkaleni's coats in need of straightening.

Danahlia cooks the rest of the lizard and Twinkaleni tries enchanting once more as Alice watches.

After another deafening pop that echoes through the forest, Alice asks, "Why does that keep happening?"

Twinkaleni sighs, "I'm not entirely sure. There could be many causes I suppose but without an instructor or instruction, I fear I may run through our entire stock of cores and still not get it right."

"Tally said she knew some pixies that know how to do that binding thing, maybe she can bring 'em next time."

Twinkaleni's ears perk up, "Well, yes, that would be an aid. I will have to ask her tomorrow when she returns."

Twinkaleni tries again despite the lateness of the hour but once Danahlia has finished cooking the girls gather into the cave for the night. Danahlia brings the roasted lizard in with them so no scavengers come for it, making the cave smell of slightly burnt meat.

For the next several days, the girls enjoy their time at their new home. The pixies come frequently, bringing with them their animal friends and a bounty of fruits. The trio often ventures around at Tally and Shae's request to clear areas of various things, mostly jellies. Sometimes they'll bring down something edible and enjoy meat, or ant, and once a very large egg that seemed to have been abandoned for no reason at all. When at camp, Twinkaleni will practice enchantment. With the help of a young pixie binder, still learning himself, the cores don't explode anymore, merely melt into black quickly hardening puddles.

For a time, Danahlia and Alice try to make things such as rope, clothes, and a few simple tools. Now, they were having a contest to see who could make a functional bow and arrows. Both girls had seen others using them at some point, but had never used them themselves, and thus, on fairly even terms, they try their hand at crafting their own.

It takes a great deal of effort to come up with materials from scratch, but they do their best and share their tools. Though this *was* a contest and so whenever one felt she had stumbled onto something good, she would often jealously guard it from the other. Twinkaleni stays out of this as much as she can but is often made to keep their secrets. Whenever one felt they had it, an archery contest was held and a great deal of bragging was awarded the girl who not only loosed an arrow but got nearest to the target. Neither had actually hit it yet during these bouts. Still, their efforts are rewarded with steadily better results.

During their frequent hunts, Alice notices an increasing number of the highly sought after red jellies. She thinks this curious while Danahlia is overjoyed. The Liguna constantly reminds the girls of all the things they could buy with the rare core stones and encourages Twinkaleni to improve her enchanting so she can further enhance their value.

After a battle that has earned them a few red cores, Alice asks, "Tally. What do you know about the red jellies?"

"Brought you here because of them we did. Created many are, by a taller."

"A taller? Isn't that the term you use for those like us?" Twinkaleni asks.

"Yes, but this taller, not like you it is," says Tally, looking around as if fearing even speaking of it, "Terrible this one. Hunts us and our friends all."

Tally explains that the other taller had been in the forest for some time, hunting and killing indiscriminately. He uses a bow with great skill, forcing the pixies and their animal friends to flee or perish. Fortunately, this unknown archer tends to stay in close proximity to some old ruins at the very heart of the forest.

"Why is he hunting you?" Alice asks, the girls gathering to listen.

"Some he eats, others he ends for…," the blue haired pixie searches for a word, "…joy. Laugh at every death he does, or so my kin say."

"This individual sounds incredibly dangerous. We should avoid him at all costs," Twinkaleni advises to a general agreement from Alice and Danahlia.

"But Jellybane, face him we hoped you would. Force him to leave you must," Tally says, bobbing up and down.

"Sorry, Tally, but this guy sounds like a bit much for us," Alice admits.

"But, but great warriors you are, known this is!" Tally argues.

"Perhaps if we knew more about him, we could come up with some sort of strategy. What he looks like, his capabilities, resources, behavior patterns," Twinkaleni offers.

Tally groans, "Know this I do not. We do not go near the land he stalks. Know only he is a taller and danger to all."

"You mentioned he created the red jellies?" Twinkaleni asks.

Tally flutters in tight spirals, "Some have said what he does not eat he gives to the jellies and red they become."

Twinkaleni wonders, "Why would he do this?"

"I know not," Tally replies glumly.

"Are we close to his camp?" asks Danahlia.

"The hunter's territory is not far. Face him will you?" Tally bobs cheerily.

"Uh, no. I kinda want to head back to the cave," admits Danahlia. The girls agree and Tally sags in the air.

On their way back, Tally tries to convince the girls to challenge the vile hunter and force him out of the pixies' forest. But from what they've heard so far, they have no interest in facing such a being. The blue haired pixie becomes upset and flutters off. Alice sighs, wanting to help but, like the others, is rather frightened of facing this unknown menace.

"Why would some guy be living in the forest?" Danahlia ponders aloud.

"Perhaps a hermit or someone seeking refuge from the outside as we are," Twinkaleni suggests.

"What're we gonna to do? What if we run into this guy?" Alice asks as they reach their camp.

It's late in the afternoon and the girls are tired. They've managed to gather a small larder of food consisting mostly of giant ants and some fruit they've managed to keep from eating. Danahlia collects a decent sized ant from their stores as Twinkaleni lights the fire.

Danahlia breaks the ant into two parts and sticks a spit through both, "Maybe we can take him. You can't be that tough if you need to pick on pixies and small ferals."

"We should avoid this man for now. We know too little. Perhaps the pixies can gather more information on him," Twinkaleni advises, sitting down by the fire.

The girls are amid their discussion when Shae appears, followed by their usual fruit delivery service. The younger pixies have returned as well and after flocking around Danahlia for her greatly embellished tale of the day's battles with the jellies, they flutter around the camp. Shae informs them that she ran into Tally on her way there and wonders what to do about the hunter.

"We wanna help, but we're not sure what we can do," Alice says, a few pixies perched on her head.

Shae bobs, "Understand I do. Hinder us the Jellies and others may, but rarely can they do us true harm. The hunter is different, an ender it is, a threat even to the Jellybane."

The younger pixies share their knowledge of the hunter, which mostly amounts to them all saying he is dangerous in slightly different ways.

Twinkaleni waves away some of the pixies to add, "We may be able to come up with some sort of plan but we must be better informed. We will need your help if we are to have any chance of ridding the forest of this hunter."

"Difficult this may be. Keep far from the hunter we do," says Shae.

"We need spies," Danahlia asserts, taking the cooked ant off the fire.

"Exactly. Perhaps you can ask your people and friends to gather information about the hunter. The more we know, the better we can plan for an encounter," says Twinkaleni, still waving off a few pixies that seem to have made a game of seeing who can stay on her great round ears the longest.

Shae says she will try to do this but seems apprehensive.

"Relax, it's just one guy. How bad could he be?" assures Danahlia, cracking open an ant segment.

Chapter 9

Hunter Hunting

The following morning, Tally returns with Shae and the sisters announce that they have been talking to all of their kindred to find out as much as they can about the hunter. More than a little seems to be exaggerated, such as the hunter is the size of a tree, but some of the information is more valuable. As near as they can figure, the hunter has been in the forest for several months. He is a large male taller. Though considering the source, large seems subjective. He is mostly known for attacking with a bow but has been known to set various traps. The pixies have managed to avoid him since they'd taken measures to stay away from the ruins the hunter inhabits, and he rarely leaves their vicinity. Shae also tells the girls that she has managed to get volunteers to spy on the hunter and has already sent a few to do so.

More days pass with the girls continuing their usual activities while staying clear of the hunter's territory. The pixies bring them new information about the hunter, revealing he has dark gray fur and a long furless tail, though often wears a hood. He also carries a long knife along with his bow and has been spotted making his own arrows. They confirm he is alone and sleeps in the ruins, which are rigged with various simple traps that, according to them, are too large for pixies or ferals.

Twinkaleni asks, "Shae, do you think you could get someone to cut his bow's string? I think that would greatly hamper his capabilities."

"Yeah, if he can't hunt, maybe he'll go hungry and leave," Danahlia says hopefully.

"A nice thought, but we can't count on it," says Twinkaleni, "You and Alice have proven a bow string can be manufactured from local flora, and such an experienced hunter would no doubt be able to replace theirs. No, the cutting of the bow string would have to happen in sync with any attempt to strike out at this individual, if it comes to it."

"A great risk this would be, but do it we will if it will aid in freeing the forest from the hunter," Shae assures them.

"At least we know there's only one. Who knows, maybe he doesn't understand the damage he's doing. Maybe we could try reasoning with him," Alice suggests.

"I say we ambush 'im. If it's just one, I think we can take 'im," puts in Danahlia, pounding a fist into the palm of her hand.

"Calm down, Danny, Alice may be onto something. I think It would be best to avoid violence if at all possible," Twinkaleni reasons.

The Murin mage expresses her interest in having multiple plans, each with contingencies. She manages to come up with a surprising number of ideas, all with numerous variables, most of which seem needlessly complex to her companions.

After a while, Alice yawns, raising her hand as Twinkaleni is going over the pros and cons of yet another plan, "I'm leanin' toward ambushin' 'im too. If Shae can get the bow string cut, we can hit him when he goes out looking for materials to make a new one. He won't have a bow and won't be prepared for a fight."

Twinkaleni nods, "Yes, but that's assuming he doesn't already have some prepared." She looks to Shae, "Do you think you could get someone to check his supplies, so we know exactly what this hunter has to work with?"

Shae sags, "Apologies, Master Orbear, we have not yet dared to get so close. The danger is too great."

"Twinkie, we can't keep asking these guys to put their lives on the line if we aren't willin' to do the same," asserts Danahlia.

"But-" Twinkaleni starts though Danahlia interrupts.

"I know you're scared. I'm scared. Alice, you scared?"

"Yeah, I'm scared," the young Tokala admits.

"See, but we can do this. We outnumber 'im three to one. You have magic. And with the pixies on our side, we can't lose," Danahlia assures Twinkaleni, putting both hands on the diminutive mage's shoulders.

The small mouse looks up at the Liguna, "But how can you be so certain?"

"Because I know you're gonna to be watchin' my back," Danahlia replies easily.

Twinkaleni smiles and lets out a breath, "Alright then."

Confidence bolstered, Twinkaleni outlines a fairly simple plan that the girls can execute the very next day.

The pixies cheer and dart away, eager to tell their kin of the Jellybane's plan as well as recruit volunteers for their own dangerous part in it. The girls go over the plan several times until Danahlia, bored and tired, calls an end to it. The pixies are to infiltrate the hunter's lair and disable the hunter's bow while simultaneously sabotaging as much of his supplies and traps as they can tonight. In the morning, if he ventures out to replenish his stocks, that will be the opportunity to attack. The pixies will keep an eye on his whereabouts and relay the information to the girls in the field so they can ambush him, unaware and unprepared. They do not intend to use violence unless necessary, but between Alice's sword, Danahlia's spear, and Twinkaleni's magic, they figure the hunter will be too pressed to mount any effective resistance. Plan made, the girls go to bed early to be well rested for their hunt of the hunter.

They wake up before dawn the next morning and eat well. Going over their plan again, they pack light for their mission. Once ready, Tally leads the girls deeper into the forest and into the hunter's domain. Their own bows still too unreliable to bring, Alice and Danahlia only take their battle proven arms. Shae reports that her infiltration team has managed to damage the hunters bow and even disarm several traps. The green haired pixie and another now track the hunter as he leaves his camp with nothing but his knife.

The girls cheer their early success as they advance on their unsuspecting enemy, still a fair distance away according to their pixie intelligence. They stick to the formation outlined by Twinkaleni which has Alice and Danahlia side by side upfront while the mage takes the rear. The plan is to surprise the hunter, distract him with sword and spear and then hit him with magic from afar if need be.

It's nearly noon when Shae's partner dismally reports that Shae has been captured. Tally shrieks, darting away with the other after her sister. The girls run and call after them for a short while but quickly loose the swift pixies, leaving them blind in an unfamiliar part of the dense forest.

"Ticks, what do we do now?" Danahlia whispers harshly, not wanting to risk giving them away. The last report said they were not far from the hunter's position.

"We gotta help Shae. Let's just keep goin' this way, maybe we'll run into 'em soon," says Alice, looking around nervously.

"Keep on your guard, we may run into the hunter at any time," Twinkaleni advises.

They advance, weapons at the ready. The knowledge of such a dangerous individual lurking nearby turns the once comforting forest into a world of danger. Their pace slows as they freeze at every sound, their breaths catching, only to realize it's nothing time and again. Alice keeps her ears perked, trying to listen past the rustle of forest dwellers to hear any sign of the hunter. There are an abundance of jellies in the area, and more red ones than they've seen yet. The trio avoids them as best they can while trying to stay quite.

After over an hour, Danahlia groans, "We should've seen somethin' by now." Twinkaleni shushes her but she goes on, "We're probably not even goin' in the right direction anymore."

"What'd you wanna do?" asks Alice.

"Guess that depends on what you're tryin' ta find," a male's voice says from behind.

The girls jump, turning to see a tall lanky man with similar features to Twinkaleni, though with a longer more angular muzzle and darker colors. They can compare them easily since the man is holding the mouse mage against his thighs with a long curved knife at her neck, his other hand over her mouth. He has a hood over his head and wears simple dirty garments with a menacing grin.

In a mix of anger and fear, Alice and Danahlia raise their weapons, Danahlia demanding he let Twinkaleni go. The man lifts the Murin's head, holding the knife against her throat close enough that the some of the edge is obstructed by her light gray fur. Twinkaleni's hands move about uncertainly as she desperately tries to remain calm.

"I think I'll hold on to this one," he sneers and then lifts a dark gray eyebrow, "Mighty fine sword you got there, little lady. Go ahead and drop it, sheath and all. You too, Smoothie."

The girls look to each other and Twinkaleni tries to say something but her voice in muffled by the man's hand. Terrified, they drop their weapons.

"That's it, now just turn 'round and start walkin' the way you were," the man instructs.

Too frightened to come up with anything else, the girls do as they're bid.

The man picks up their weapons, slinging Alice's sword over his shoulder while using Danahlia's spear to prod Twinkaleni along, threatening to impale the little mouse if they try anything. They are threatened or simply jabbed any time they try to look back or speak, which makes their march to the man's camp an uncomfortable and silent one.

The hunter has chosen to lair in what must have once been an impressive fort or keep. All that remains of it now though are one or two barely serviceable looking structures surrounded by scattered gray, moss covered stone. There were clearly other structures once but they have long since collapsed in on themselves and appear as piles of rubble framed with a few bits of stubborn wall. Plant life bursts forth from much of it making Alice think that these ruins were from some long forgotten age.

The Tokala slows to look around and is prodded by the spear before she can take much in, but around a small fire, crumpled into a heap, is a tattered and stained tabard with a symbol she recognizes from the messenger who came to gather men, her father among them, for the war several years ago. A golden lion.

"You're a soldier?" Alice can't help asking.

Her question is rewarded with another sharp jab and a harsh, "Shut up!"

Alice yips, a spot on her upper back burning hot as her fur moistens with blood. She grits her teeth against the pain and remains silent.

They're prodded into a large, partially intact hall where there are more than a few red jellies wobbling about. Short stone walls, somewhat like the one Twinkaleni had the girls build at their cave, have been erected to keep the jellies contained in pens of a sort. Alice finds this very curious but keeps quiet, not wanting to risk another stab. As they're led through, a wooden table with a few assorted items comes into view. On it are Tally and the other pixie trying to open a cloth sack.

They just manage to get the string keeping it closed untied as Danahlia warns, "Guys! Get outta here!"

Danahlia is given a hard whack on the head with the butt of her own spear. The sound of the blow echoes through the cavernous hall and she falls to her knees. The pixies look up as Shae pops free of the sack. The three pixies immediately dart away and out of a hole in the questionable roof.

"Damn flyin' devils," the man snarls and then begins kicking Danahlia in the back, "Get up, Smoothie, this ain't the place to rest."

"Leave her alone!" Alice shouts, both her and Twinkaleni kneeling at Danahlia's side.

"You want one too?" the man threatens, raising the spear once more, "Get 'er up, NOW!"

The Liguna manages to find her feet and the trio is prodded to a small room with a weathered but still functional wooden door that looks to have been hastily repaired. The dark room has no visible windows and its only furnishing is a bed of grasses and some cloth, perhaps where their captor had been sleeping. The girls are roughly shoved inside the room and plunged into blackness when the door is slammed behind them.

Danahlia immediately begins pounding on the door, screaming, "LET US OUT!"

The door opens and the man, having pulled back his hood, reveals himself to be a Rotan, one of the rat people, the small naked pink ears on his head a dead giveaway. He gives Danahlia a back handed slap that sends her spinning to the hard, stone floor.

"Danny!" Alice and Twinkaleni cry together, collapsing beside her. The Liguna is more enraged than hurt and has to be held down while the rat man glares at them.

"Better keep that one in check, girls, that little outburst just cost you your supper," he smirks and closes the door once more. A moment later the sound of something heavy being pushed against it can be heard.

"Ticks! What are we gonna to do now?" Danahlia grumbles angrily, a spot of blood dripping from a break in her lip.

"The first thing we *must* do is escape this room," Twinkaleni asserts.

In agreement, the girls fan out to look for anything they can use. The Murin mage starts to voice her thoughts in a sort of rambling checklist, "He is keeping us alive, which means he plans to do something with us, which gives us some time to come up with a plan. It looks like he was sleeping in here, which means this is one of the more secure rooms in this ruin, which will make escape difficult, but also means his supplies and thus ours are likely close by, perhaps even just outside. The pixies know we're here and may attempt a rescue, though I don't imagine they will be able to do much without us. There are no windows and we have no way to contact them. There is no lock on the door, but something heavy was placed to keep us in. We can't see, there is no light..."

"He doesn't know you can use magic," Alice whispers, crawling around and feeling with her hands to find the bed.

"Yeah, maybe give 'im a face full o' fire the next time he opens that door," Danahlia adds, picking up a fist sized stone that's broken loose from the wall.

Only the door doesn't open again. Twinkaleni rambles on and on to the point it seems strange even for her. Alice finds the small mouse in the dark, shivering terribly as she tosses out an endless stream of possibilities, probabilities, and variables.

"Twinkaleni? Twinkaleni?!" Alice calls to her but the Murin just keeps going on. "Danny, I think there's somethin' wrong with 'er."

Danahlia finds them and they both run their hands over their friend's shivering form. She's curled into a ball, her arms and legs, tucked in tight.

"Twinkie? What's wrong? Snap out of it!" Danahlia demands, giving her a shake.

Alice stops the Liguna and puts her arms around the smaller girl, holding her close, "She's terrified."

They both hold her, putting their cheeks against the shivering girl's.

"Can't say I blame 'er. We're not doin' too well right now," Danahlia says from Alice's left.

They both stroke the little mouse's fur and tell her soothing things to try to calm her. After a while, she doesn't shake so badly and eventually stops babbling.

They sit in the darkness petting Twinkaleni's soft fur until she stops completely, she then states, "We have to get out of here."

"Workin' on it," Danahlia tells her with a hug.

"Are you ok? What happened?" Alice asks, taking her small furless hand into her own.

"The Order, they... I'm sorry, it just, brought back some bad memories is all," Twinkaleni apologizes, gripping Alice's hand tight.

Danahlia kisses the little mouse on the forehead, "Well, if you're done freakin' out, we could use some light."

"Yes, yes of course. Estraleete."

After being in pitch blackness for so long, Twinkaleni's tiny ball of light is blinding and Alice sees even the mage look away.

"It must be dark now, this feels like moon and starlight," the Murin says as they take in the room.

There really isn't much to see, cobwebs around the ceiling corners, stone walls in need of repair, and the bed. The door doesn't look overly imposing and Danahlia pushes on it. The door opens a fraction of an inch before being stopped by something. Alice joins her and then, putting out the light, so does Twinkaleni. They all push with everything they have and the obstruction begins to slide the slightest bit, until something clatters noisily on the other side.

"Hey!" the man shouts from what sounds like a short distance away. The distinct sound of footsteps closing on them follows as he snarls, "Get away from the door!" before the door is slammed shut again.

"Let us out you flea bitten-" Danahlia starts but Alice clamps a hands over her mouth.

"I'm sorry sir, we didn't mean to upset you. Please, will you let us out?" Alice tries as they hear the man picking up whatever fell.

"No chance, just sit in there and shut up," he growls.

"How long do you intend to keep us in here? This seems like your own room. Wouldn't you want to move us somewhere else so you can at least sleep in your own bed?" Twinkaleni calls through the door. The man doesn't respond. "Our parents will come looking for us if we're not home soon."

He barks a laugh, "Let 'em, nothin' but women, cripples, and codgers left anyway. All the men are off fightin'."

Danahlia muffles something but Alice keeps her hands over the angry Liguna's mouth to says, "Except for you?"

"Aye, 'cept for me," he replies and they can hear a smile in his tone.

"Please, we meant you no harm. We're monster hunters, just collecting core stones from the jellies to trade in town," explains Alice.

"Shut your mouths and stay put or you won't be gettin' any breakfast neither," he says disinterestedly, his voice carrying from farther away.

Danahlia beats her rock against the door a few times before Twinkaleni cries, "Stop it, Danny!"

The Liguna jerks free of Alice's grip, "Why?! He's not gonna let us out anyway! Maybe we can rile 'im up enough to come in here."

"Or he may simply leave us in here to starve. If he thinks we are being obedient, perhaps he will come in to give us food or water at some point. That will be our best chance," Twinkaleni whispers harshly.

Resigning, Danahlia puts her back to the wall and slides down to a sit. The others join her and in the darkness, Twinkaleni offers a plan. It's to wait until morning, or whenever the vile hunter intends to feed them, and then attack the moment he opens the door. With luck, he will have his hands full, probably with a weapon and their food, which will leave him defenseless to Twinkaleni's magic. When she strikes, Danahlia and Alice try to slip past and escape or attack, whichever seems feasible at the time.

In agreement, the girls wait. Alice manages to find a decent sized stone too and hefts it, her stomach rumbling with the others.

"What're you gonna to hit 'im with?" Alice asks Twinkaleni.

"I have no qualms about giving him 'a face full of fire,'" the Murin replies.

"What do you think he's doin' out here?" Danahlia wonders aloud, her ear to the door.

"I believe he is a deserter," the little mage suggests.

"A what?" Alice asks.

"A deserter, someone who flees their obligation to the army. It would explain the tabard we saw outside and why he is hiding so far from civilization. If caught by the army, he would be harshly punished, perhaps even executed. This is most likely why he has imprisoned us as well. He fears we will tell others of his location," Twinkaleni explains.

"Maybe we can use that," Danahlia murmurs.

"I don't see how since we're already imprisoned," Twinkaleni says glumly, "We cannot get a message out and he knows that even if we had parents looking for us this deep in the forest, they'd likely be a few women at best, not men, and certainly not soldiers. He has little to worry about."

"I don't wanna sit here doin' nothin' but hope he decides to feed us in the mornin'," Danahlia whispers irately.

"There's the bed," Alice motions, even though no one can see in the dark.

Twinkaleni nods, "Yes, I think Alice has the right of it. The best thing we can do is get some sleep so we are fresh to act tomorrow."

"Fine," Danahlia grumbles and they blindly make their way to the rooms only furnishing.

The bed isn't large and smells rather unpleasant, but is infinitely more comfortable than the cold, stone floor. The girls huddle together atop it and try to get some rest. It isn't easy, being in a strange and dangerous place, hungry, thirsty, and scared, but Alice finds comfort knowing she does not have to endure this alone. Snuggling in close to her friends, she eventually falls asleep.

Sometime later, Alice is bugged by something moving on her muzzle. She slaps at it lazily, waking herself up, and hearing a little cry. Suddenly a light blossoms on her nose and Tally gasps, "Jellybane?" from under her hand.

She lets the little pixie free and whispers, "Tally? I'm so glad to see you. How'd you get in here?"

"Tally?" Twinkaleni groans while Danahlia snores on.

"Slipped under the door I did, while the hunter sleeps," the little pixie says, fluttering up, her blue glow blindingly bright in the darkness.

"Did you bring anyone else with you?" Alice asks.

"Many others, even Ashbel, one of our elders, has come. Set fire to the hunter's things he will. The time is now. Break free from this place you must," Tally explains excitedly while Twinkaleni claps her hands on Danahlia's cheeks until she wakes up.

"Huh? Wha? Tally?" Danahlia mumbles.

"Get up, Danny. The pixies are breaking us out," Twinkaleni whispers as she hops out of bed.

"Do you know where my sword is outside?" Alice asks, using Tally's light to find her way to the door.

"Yes, on a table it is, burn it will not, but close to the flames it will be, see it you will."

Alice presses her ear to the door to listen but hears nothing. The others join her as she asks, "When're they gonna start?"

"Look, begun they have," Tally says, landing by the slit at the bottom of the door and crawling out. Flickering orange light begins to seep from under it, then they hear the hunter shouting curses and scrambling about.

"Let's get outta here. On three, we push," Danahlia orders. They slam their shoulder in sync into the door, forcing it to budge but barely an inch at a time. Whatever lay atop the heavy obstruction clatters to the floor again as the chaos outside continues. "Come on guys, PUSH!"

Danahlia manages to get an arm out as the door cracks open and uses the frame as a brace to shove with everything she has. The door opens a bit more and she gets a taloned foot digging into the wooden door as well, her thigh flexing hard as she shoves. The slim opening lets them see the hunter rampaging about, pixies fluttering high around him.

"Filthy flyin' devils!" they hear him snarl as he slashes with his knife at the pixies darting at his head and zipping away. "No! You get back in there or I'll cut all your throats right here!" he roars, turning away from his tiny harassers to charge at the door.

"Twinkie, GO!" Danhalia shouts. The little mouse girl crawls under the taller girl's leg and out of their prison. Alice squeezes out right behind her as Danahlia struggles to hold the door open by herself.

The hall is alight with dancing orange flames where several fires burn. The hunter is bearing down on them, knife raised to strike when Twinkaleni shouts, "Feasta!"

A burst of fire flies free of her palm and into the man's face. He screams in surprise and pain. The attack is short lived, however, as he barrels blindly into Twinkaleni and Alice, sending them both tumbling away. The mouse mage hits the wall to Danahlia's side hard while Alice falls into one of the jelly enclosures and is nearly grabbed by one of the monsters. She manages to roll away, getting to her feet as the man howls his fury.

The fox girl sees her sword on a table and has to run, leaping over a short stone wall to get to it. Not bothering to take the sheath, she pulls free her blade and dashes back to her friends. The rat man has regained some sense of focus, still holding his scorched face with one hand as he targets a dazed Twinkaleni.

"WITCH! I'll gut you all for this!" he snarls down at the small Murin.

The stones and table leaning into the door have rolled back into place, pinning Danahlia against it and the frame. She squirms in obvious discomfort, one leg and arm stuck in the small room while the rest of her hangs out helplessly in the hall, reaching desperately for the man. Twinkaleni lies on the floor, a tiny pink hand raised in a feeble attempt to defend herself as the man pulls back his arm to stab her with his knife. Danahlia screams.

Alice does too, hurling her sword with both hands, knowing there is no other way. If she missed, she and her friends were going to die horribly at the Rotan's hands. But she doesn't. The blade sticks into the meat of the man's thigh and he howls in agony, falling to one knee. He turns to Alice who freezes under the mad rage pouring from his one unburnt eye. The rat man lifts his knife overhead to throw but gasps as Danahlia, still pinned, manages to pull the sword from his leg only to ram it into his back with enough force that the point emerges from his chest. He watches in disbelief as blood blooms on his tunic. He then looks to Alice, his gaze radiating malice and blame before he collapses.

After a few shallow breathes, Alice overcomes her shock and forces herself to move. She pushes over the table and various stones keeping the door closed on Danahlia. The Liguna squeezes through, stepping over the man's body to check on Twinkaleni. They all manage to come out of their ordeal with only bumps, bruises, and a few minor cuts. The valiant pixies flutter around the girls, some cheering the fall of the hunter as his meager belongings burn.

After starting a more controlled fire and putting out the others, the girls flop against a wall together. With the adrenaline leaving their bodies, they find themselves very tired and hungry.

An orange pixie introduces himself as Ashbelodin. Despite his title of elder, he doesn't appear very elderly at all. Only slightly taller than the average pixie, his features are youthful and strong. He was the one who set the fires and thanks the trio graciously for their part in bringing down the greatly feared hunter. He then leads most of the other pixies away to spread word. Tally and Shae stay behind with the exhausted trio assuring the girls there will be a great celebration.

After a few hours of sleep, the weary heroes are awakened when hundreds of pixies swarm into the hall along with many of their animal friends. The girls are given more of the Niurha tree's precious revitalizing nectar and are soon able to join in a grand party. The animals bring food as the pixies dance and sing joyous melodies while the girls fill their bellies. When they feel up to it, the girls clear the room full of red jellies, showing off their skills for a cheering crowd. By morning, a pyre has been built and the Rotan and his remaining belongings are burned to help cleanse his taint from the forest.

Found among his things is a journal that Twinkaleni spares from the fire. Based on a change from writing to doodles, the tattered little book seems to have belonged to another before the Rotan got hold of it. The hunter had drawn and written in charcoal, information mostly pertaining to the forest. There are a few simple maps showing the locations of various resources such as water, where certain plants were found, as well as food. Mostly through symbols, the journal also informs the girls that the hunter had likely intended to use the jellies in some sort of attack on nearby villages by luring them with food. He had listed various plants, animals, and even pixies that were used as bait followed by how well they worked. Knowing this helps Alice feel a little less conflicted about their need to put an end to the rat man.

Being an improvement over their cave, the ruin is cleaned out over the next days and all the girl's belongings are brought to their new home. From this centralized location, the trio continues to help reclaim territory from the jellies, much to the appreciation of the pixies, who, along with their feral friends, continue to supply plenty of delicious fruit to the effort.

After a time, the heroic trio is asked to come to a celebration in their honor as true friends of the pixies. Tally, Shae, Airi, and a number of others escort them to what the pixies say is one of the last Niurha trees in the forest.

The tree is a magnificent sight. The trunk is as thick as a small house with surface roots reaching far in all directions. The bark of the tree is pale and luminous, much like the pixies own skin. Its branches reach far and high, the ends of each tipped in an abundance of rounded leaves. On many of the branches hang small spherical structures that must be the pixies' dwellings. They look like balls of leaves kept together by intricately weaving supple branches, many of which have pixies emerging to greet their guests. Animals, including all they have seen and many they have not, travel about in the great tree's branches and the others it joins with.

Great piles of fruits, nuts, berries, seeds, and juices are laid out on piles of leaves for all to enjoy. Many of the usually skittish ferals come up to Alice and smell her, many even letting her pet them. The pixies that know the trio best tell stories of their adventures, there is also singing, dancing, and of course, plenty of eating. The festivities continue until a silence is called for the main event.

All watch as the elder pixie binder gathers his pupils and asks for Alice's sword. The young Tokala rises and lays it on the ground in a clearing as directed. The pixies most gifted in binding hover in a circle around the weapon and begin singing an unusual song while sprinkling glowing green powered from tiny pouches at their waists. Tally tells them that the powder was made from the cores of the defeated jellies and as they watch, some of the falling powder sticks to the blade, making it glow as well.

As the pixies swirl around, singing their undulating melody, more and more of the powder flies onto the sword, steadily intensifying its glow. Even in the light of day, the glow becomes intense at the climax of the magical working, but then begins to die down as the pixie's song slows and ends. The binder pixies go silent, their tiny shoulders slumping from the effort, as they flutter away to leave the elder pixie hovering over the weapon. He waves for Alice to approach. Like Ashbel, this elder doesn't look old at all either, his hair is a golden yellow and he too possesses features of youth and strength. He smiles tiredly and gestures for Alice to take up her sword.

When she does the blade glows green once more, similarly to core stones. The elder binder then says, "Many jellies you have slain with this blade, and we hope, many more you will."

"We definitely will," assures a grinning Alice, looking her sword up and down, "Why's it glowing?" The general appearance is exactly the same, but now it pulses with a faint green light.

"Bind the essence of core stones to it, we did," the elder explains, "Taint it the jellies cannot."

Alice doesn't quite understand what he means but her tail wags knowing she has been given something incredible. She thanks the elder who bows and raises his arms to his people. The pixies cheer and even the ferals make various noises as she brings her sword back to her friends. Twinkaleni touches the simple crossguard and is impressed with the magic it now holds.

Alice hands the glowing weapon to Danahlia who examines it approvingly, "Wags. I wonder if they can make my spear glow, too."

"Danny," Twinkaleni chides, "it has clearly taken a great deal from these people to do this for us."

"I know. I meant like, later," she says, handing the weapon back with a smirk.

"Enchanted weapons are a rare thing, Alice. All the ones I have ever read about had great names along with great legends. Perhaps you could give yours a name to mark the beginning of your own," Twinkaleni suggests.

Alice had never named a sword before, but there is only one name she can think of, only one that is both distinct and memorable, "Alright. I think I'll call it, Jellybane."

Epilogue

The girls live happily in the forest for a time with their pixie and animal friends. After some work, the ruins turn out to be a wonderful place to stay, both safe and dry while being in the heart of the forest. This central location makes it an ideal staging area for the girls to help reclaim the forest for those who dwell within it. They fight many battles with the jellies, taking back groves of trees, streams, springs, and ponds all over the forest. During this campaign, Alice finds that her newly enchanted sword would glow when jellies were nearby.

They also discover another rather convenient new trait of Jellybane. It now never needed to be cleaned. Each time jelly goo, or anything else, would stain the sword, the blade would glow. The goo would then dry and flake away, leaving the blade gleaming as if freshly polished.

The girls manage to gather an impressive hoard of core stones to eventually trade, though for the time being the treasures simply gathered into a large pile. Twinkaleni chips away at this while she practices her enchanting. Pixie magic works differently than her own and even with some help, she only ever made one core glow brighter the way she wanted, though she admits it was more luck than design.

Their time among the pixies is cut short, however, when a taller is said to have entered the forest. The pixies often reported on dangerous sightings such as giant ants, spiders, and lizards, sometimes asking the girls to dispatch them if they posed a particular threat.

But as this taller is being described to them, Twinkaleni gasps, "Oh no. The Order... they've come for me."

"The one you escaped from?" Alice asks.

"Yes. The triangle containing the open eye, it is the Order of Thermathrogi's symbol. I must leave," the Murin mage blurts in a panic as she rushes off to gather her things. Alice, Danahlia, Tally, and a few other pixies follow her around as she picks up her backpack to start cramming items into it.

"What do you mean, leave?" Danahlia asks, chasing the small girl around their ruin home.

"If they've tracked me this far, it can only mean they're using my tail in conjuncture with some locating enchantment. It's only a matter of time before they find their way here. I must be gone before then. You and Alice can stay, hide for a time, the pixies can keep an eye out. The Order will follow me when I leave."

"What're you talkin' about?" Alice asks, back stepping as Twinkaleni suddenly turns into her.

"I can't let them find me. I have to go, now," the Murin insists.

"Whoa, you don't think I'm gonna to let you go that easy do you?" Danahlia asserts, grabbing the little mouse by both shoulders to stop her.

Twinkaleni shakes her head, "No, Danny, stay here, if they find me..."

"You mean if they find *us*," Alice interrupts, kneeling in front of her, "We're a team, we stick together."

"Yeah, if you go, we go. Right Alice?" Danahlia asks, gripping the little mage tighter.

"Right," Alice nods.

Twinkaleni shakes her head more violently, "The Order is far too dangerous. I cannot ask you to…"

"You're not askin', we're doin', plus we're older so that's that. Let's pack, looks like we're goin' on a road trip," Danahlia orders, giving Twinkaleni a kiss atop of her head. The little mouse girl sighs and they gather what they can carry.

It takes the girls several days to reach the opposite edge of the forest from where the taller was spotted. Their forest friends provide them with guidance and food to help speed them along, while keeping close watch on the taller. Without adequate knowledge, the pixies assure the girls that it will take a great deal of time for their pursuer to find their way through their wood. Danahlia suggests the individual may give up all together, but Twinkaleni doesn't seem very confident of this.

When they reach the trees that mark the boundary of the pixie's forest, the trio says their goodbyes to their dear tiny friends, head out into the open, and onto their next adventure.

About the Author:

K.J. Bailey (Kenichiro Justin Bailey) has thus far only written the Alice Dippleblack series, but looks forward to creating more fantastical worlds.

www.ingramcontent.com/pod-product-compliance
Lightning Source LLC
Chambersburg PA
CBHW032208190626
46810CB00019B/2180